"Being [...] like living on a roller coaster

"Mitch wasn't the easiest man to live with, but just when I'd think we'd made a mistake, along would come a high." Alanna smiled at her former mother-in-law and dear friend. "Those wildly exhilarating highs were what always made me want to take another ride."

"And Jonas?" Elizabeth Cantrell asked softly.

"Life with Jonas is more peaceful. Tranquil."

Lost in thought, Alanna failed to see her fiancé standing in the doorway, a blistering scowl on his rugged features.

She made him sound boring. Worse than boring. Bland, Jonas Harte considered darkly. It hadn't been easy treating Alanna Cantrell with kid gloves. From the moment he'd met her, he'd known she was the woman he'd been waiting for all his life.

But beneath Alanna's sleek, self-assured exterior, he'd sensed a vulnerability that had made him take things slowly, courting her with an almost old-world chivalry when what he wanted to do was drag her caveman-style to the nearest bed and ravish her.

Dammit, he vowed, *he would take Alanna Cantrell on the ride of her life!*

Dear Reader,

JoAnn Ross has written a poignant love story that
we, the editors, just adore and know you will too!
Tangled Hearts is a powerful romance about a
woman torn between two lovers: the husband she
assumed was dead and the fiancé she is about to
marry. Alanna's choice is difficult, and you'll be
as torn between these two wonderful men as she
is.

When JoAnn finished *Tangled Hearts,* she
realized the story wasn't over yet; she had to
answer the question, what happens to the man
who doesn't win Alanna? His story (no, we're not
telling you who!) will be available in May 1991,
from Temptation. Don't miss *Tangled Lives!*

We'd love to hear from you about Mitch, Alanna
and Jonas. Please take the time to write to us.

The Editors
Harlequin Temptation
225 Duncan Mill Road
Don Mills, Ontario, Canada
M3B 3K9

Tangled Hearts

JoAnn Ross

Harlequin Books

TORONTO • NEW YORK • LONDON
AMSTERDAM • PARIS • SYDNEY • HAMBURG
STOCKHOLM • ATHENS • TOKYO • MILAN

Published February 1991

ISBN 0-373-25433-4

TANGLED HEARTS

Prologue

THE WARNING SIGNS had always been there. Years later, when she could look back on that fateful evening with the detachment of time, Alanna Cantrell would realize that both she and Mitch had deliberately chosen not to heed them.

Mitch, of course, had always remained steadfastly impervious to danger. His innate, devil-may-care attitude had contributed hugely to his success; it was also partly why she had fallen in love with him. Alanna had never met a man as dashing as Mitchell Cantrell. Which was why she'd permitted herself to believe him, when he assured her that their love was a talisman. A magic charm that would protect them from the madness.

It was a typically hot evening in June. The sun was a bright yellow ball, riding low on the horizon when she left her office at the American University of Beirut. Protestors marched in front of the salmon-pink American embassy next door; Alanna ignored them.

It was her first wedding anniversary, and she was determined to enjoy it. For just this one night she was going to forget that she lived in a war zone, was going to ignore the blackened, charred ruins and broken water pipes and pretend that the city was as it once had been—the Paris of the Middle East.

For this one night she was going to pretend that the *sûks*, the markets that had been reduced to rubble, were once again glittering with gold and the brilliant sheen of silk. And for this single evening she was going to make believe she didn't see the children clambering over an abandoned antiaircraft gun on the nearby beach, where a bright red Ferris wheel suggested an earlier, more carefree time.

Mitch was waiting for her on the steps of the building. She was about to fly into his arms when he suddenly pulled a colorful bouquet from behind his back.

"Tulips!" Alanna dipped her head and inhaled the sweet fragrance from the cerise, lavender and saffron-hued, cup-shaped blossoms. "They're absolutely exquisite. But how in the world did you find tulips in Beirut?"

He laughed, a deep, rumbling sound that had always possessed the power to thrill her. "It's not that hard. You simply have to know where to look."

"These must have cost a virtual fortune on the black market," she murmured, touching the velvety petals.

The fragrant flowers created a stirring of all too familiar homesickness for San Francisco. The hydrangeas would be in full blossom on Russian Hill's serpentine Lombard Street, puffy snowball-shaped blossoms of pink and white. Gardeners would be putting out the bright yellow and red zinnias at the Palace of the Legion of Honor, Golden Gate Park would be ablaze with color, and sidewalk stands would be brimming with brilliant, freshly cut flowers.

"Hey, don't worry, my little chickadee." Mitch bent down to nuzzle her neck, enjoying the soft, feminine scent of gardenias emanating from her skin. "The nest egg is intact."

Since their wedding, Alanna had been saving for a house back in the States. A large house, with plenty of room for children and a big tree in the backyard for a swing. Mitch had promised her that after this last assignment in the Middle East, he'd be ready to settle down. Personally, after having spent the last twelve months watching him work, Alanna considered that an optimistic timetable, but she wanted to be ready when—and if— her talented newsman husband suddenly became domesticated.

"Remember I told you that Pier Uttenbos's wife went home to Holland to have her baby last month?" Mitch asked.

"Of course." Alanna also recalled how the news of Pier's newborn daughter had triggered her own desire for a child. Mitch's child.

"Well, as luck would have it, he was due to return from Amsterdam today, so I asked him to bring along some flowers for my beautiful bride."

With the rigid self-honesty that had always served her well, Alanna knew that her eyes were too wide, her chin was too square, and her long brown hair was too rainwater straight to be considered beautiful. As if that wasn't enough, her skin was too pale, refusing to tan even in this land of perpetual sunshine. But every time Mitch looked at her in that special intimate way of his, she felt beautiful, desirable.

He'd been away in the south, sleeping on the ground, evading blockades, trying to avoid being killed in the cross fire that was part and parcel of the civil war. The idea that he had been thinking of her was wonderful.

"You are the most romantic man I've ever known." She knew her heart shone in her eyes as she looked up at him.

"I sure as hell didn't used to be," he admitted, thinking back to those days of hit-and-run relationships in exotic locales with women who'd been no more eager than he to settle down. "But I've discovered that it's easy to be romantic when you're married to the most delectable woman in the world." Mitch cupped her chin in his long, dark fingers and bent his head. The kiss was a brief flare of heat that ended much too soon.

"So how was your day?" he asked as they began strolling down the Avenue de Paris.

"We're still wading our way through the Peloponnesian War." Alanna tucked her arm through her husband's. The wide gold band on the ring finger of her left hand gleamed in the brilliance of the setting sun.

"That's the one between Sparta and Athens? Back in the fifth century, right?"

She grinned up at him. "Very good."

Mitch shrugged. "Being married to a classics professor, I was bound to pick up something. Besides, I took an intro classics course in my sophomore year at Stanford. So, is old Thucydides still as dry as I remember him from my college days?"

"He's a bit grim. And undeniably pessimistic, but there are times when he can display a savage wit. Anyway, we've just reached the place where Thucydides begins to realize the importance of Persia in the conflict. That local reference seems to have piqued interest."

"History is always more interesting when it hits close to home."

"I know. But that's enough classics lectures for today," she decided with a shake of her dark head. "It's not every day I celebrate my first wedding anniversary, and I refuse to spoil it with talk about the war, or Greek historians, or even the network. Years from now, when we're old and gray and sitting on our front porch watching our grandchildren playing tag in the flower beds, I want to look back and remember tonight as a special magical time."

"You and me both, babe. And with that romantic end in mind, I made reservations at the Commodore." Her fleeting frown lasted no longer than a heartbeat, but his sharp eyes—intense blue eyes that never missed a thing—caught it. "What's wrong?"

She forced a smile. "Nothing." With the probing look that made him the most effective television news interviewer in the business he studied her. "Really," Alanna insisted.

Still that long, unblinking look.

"Stop that," she complained on a laugh. "You know how I hate it when you give me your *60 Minutes* stare. Another second of that silent intimidation and I'll be confessing to the latest car bombing."

"My wife, Allie Cantrell—urban terrorist." The soft breeze from the Mediterranean Sea across the street blew a few random strands of silky brown hair against her cheek. He tenderly brushed them away.

The idea that this quiet, scholarly, delicately beautiful woman was his wife never ceased to amaze him. Marriage had never held any interest for Mitchell Cantrell. Not that he had anything against the institution of matrimony, he'd sometimes quipped, it was just that he didn't want to spend his life in an institution. Besides, he'd always been too busy running to the world's hot spots to ever consider settling down.

But that was before he returned home from Lebanon for his father's funeral and discovered that the girl next door had matured into an extremely lovely young woman.

"If you really don't want to go to the Commodore, I suppose we can try the Summerland," he said. "We haven't been there since it reopened after last year's shelling."

Alanna shook her head. "The Commodore's fine. It's just that—"

"Since the press hangs out there, you're afraid we won't be left alone long enough for me to play with your leg beneath the tablecloth."

Alanna felt color drift into her cheeks. Twelve months and he could still make her want him with a single word, a wickedly raised eyebrow, the crooked smile that had contributed to *Cosmopolitan* magazine's readers voting Mitchell Cantrell the sexiest newsman on television for the past five years.

"That's part of it."

"My darling bride." He drew her into his arms and smiled down at her uplifted face. "Did you really think that after having been away for two long and celibate weeks I'd want to share my gorgeous wife with a bunch of oversexed, half-drunk reporters?"

"I had hoped we could be alone," she admitted, damning the blush that was burning her skin.

He ran his knuckles tenderly, possessively, down her flaming cheek. "And we will be. Because it just so happens that your remarkably clever and extremely horny husband has booked the honeymoon suite for the entire weekend." He waggled his eyebrows in a purely lustful fashion. "Where he has every intention of spending the next two days—and nights—ravishing his wife in every conceivable fashion. And a few inconceivable ones, as well."

Forgetting that they were on a public street, she flung her arms around his neck. "I love you, Mr. Cantrell."

"Not as much as I love you, Mrs. Cantrell," he answered. "But if we don't keep walking, Allie, my sweet, I may embarrass us both by dragging you down onto that warm sand and having my way with you right here and now."

He always made her feel so sexy. So wanted. Alanna laughed and ran her fingers through his sun-gilded blond hair. "Promises, promises."

They continued walking, hand in hand. When they reached the corner, Mitch stopped to buy two shiny red apples, individually cushioned in purple tissue paper, from a pushcart vendor. "For dessert," he explained as he handed Alanna one of the apples.

"I thought I was dessert," she complained prettily.

"Ah, but even an incomparable lover such as myself needs occasional sustenance to keep his strength up."

She was about to suggest he'd certainly never given any indication of tiring during their lovemaking before, when a bronze car suddenly pulled up to the curve and came to a stop, with an earsplitting squeal of brakes.

Three men armed with automatic rifles burst from the vehicle. Before Alanna could understand what was happening, they shoved Mitch roughly into the back seat and tore off down the Rue Bliss.

Comprehension came raining down upon her like a hail of cluster bombs. Dropping to her knees in the street, where only moments before the car—and her husband— had been, Alanna began to scream.

1

June
Five years later

THE NIGHT WAS COOL. The fog had come in, wrapping the city lights in a soft misty blanket that dulled their brilliance. A breeze off San Francisco Bay pushed the silvery tendrils of fog into the hollows of each of the city's forty-three hills. When the lonely sound of a foghorn echoed across the icy waters, Alanna shivered.

"I thought I'd find you out here." Elizabeth Cantrell, Mitch's mother, came out onto the balcony with an ivory cashmere shawl, which she wrapped around Alanna's bare shoulders. "It's much too chilly a night to be out without a wrap, dear."

"I wasn't thinking." Alanna drew the shawl more tightly around herself, aware that the ultrachic saleswoman at Saks had only assured her that the emerald silk, off-the-shoulder cocktail dress enhanced her eyes and showed off her slender figure. She had not promised that the dress would keep Alanna warm.

"Oh, I think the problem was that you were thinking too much," the older woman countered.

Alanna didn't answer. Instead, unable to meet what she knew would be a sympathetic gaze laced with pity, she pretended a sudden interest in the pyramid-shaped Transamerica building that was thrusting its way through the fog. From the apartment, muffled by the insulated glass doors, came the sounds of a party in full swing.

"You've nothing to feel guilty about, Alanna," Elizabeth said quietly.

Alanna turned toward her, battling with her conflicting emotions. "Don't you think I keep telling myself that? But sometimes, just when I realize I'm actually having a good time, I'll think of Mitch and..."

She stopped, unable to push the words past the enormous lump in her throat. "Oh, God," she whispered. "It's still so hard. After all this time."

Elizabeth put a beringed hand on Alanna's arm. "Alanna, dear, you can't blame yourself for Mitch's death."

"He came back a day early, so we wouldn't miss our anniversary," Alanna said flatly. "If he hadn't been on that street corner at that precise moment—"

"They would have kidnapped him at some other place. Some other time."

Alanna shook her head. "We don't know that," she insisted softly. "Not for certain."

Elizabeth's eyes were resolutely dry. After shedding innumerable tears for her son over the years, she'd made the decision to get on with her life. Something she'd thought Alanna was doing, too. Perhaps she'd been wrong.

"Darling, the State Department told you five long years ago that those fanatics were determined to capture Mitch. There was nothing you could have done that would have changed things."

"I could have insisted that we come home to San Francisco before the kidnapping. I could have refused to go to Lebanon with him in the first place."

"And do you honestly believe that would have stopped my son from going to Beirut?"

Alanna sighed. "No." She dragged her fingers through her chin-length hair. "Nothing could have kept Mitch from chasing down a story." She didn't even want to think how many times he'd gone into occupied territories, how many times he'd broken curfew in his never-ending search for the news.

Elizabeth gave her a long, level look. Alanna's sleek cut framed her face accenting her wide eyes and making the distress they reflected even more noticeable. "It's been nearly five years since he was taken hostage, Alanna. Three years since his captors released that photograph."

Three years ago, Mitch's "holy war" captors had released a statement, announcing Mitchell Cantrell's execution for high crimes against Islam. Accompanying the statement was a photograph of a man's body, riddled with machine-gun holes. Although the photograph had been too blurry for positive identification, there had been enough solid evidence for the State Department to declare Alanna's husband dead, despite the fact that his body had never been recovered.

"You've grieved long enough, Alanna. It's time for you to get on with your life."

"I know, but—"

"Don't tell me that you're having second thoughts about marrying Jonas?"

Jonas Harte was her older brother's best friend. As well as the architect she'd hired nine months ago to refurbish her Queen Anne Victorian home. He was also the man who'd managed to do what no one else had been able to do since that long-ago June night in Beirut. In his own calm, unrelenting way, Jonas had convinced Alanna that it was time for a new beginning.

"Of course not."

"Good. Because he's a wonderful man, Alanna."

"I know."

"And I'd say that, even if he hadn't agreed to let your former mother-in-law give you an engagement party. Although I do wish you'd have allowed me to tell my guests the real reason they're here tonight."

"I'd like to put off the press blitz as long as possible," Alanna murmured. "And, for the record, Jonas knows that you're much more than my mother-in-law."

When Alanna's mother, Mary, had died of cancer the summer Alanna turned twelve, Elizabeth Cantrell, next-door neighbor and Mary Fairfield's best friend, had immediately stepped in to act as surrogate mother. She'd guided the young girl through the stormy teen years, explained menstruation as something uniquely female and wonderful, accompanied Alanna on her first bra-shopping expedition, dried her tears when she'd been stood up for the junior prom and surprised her with a breathtakingly beautiful white organza dress for her high school graduation.

She had always been there for Alanna, offering advice when needed, or simply lending a sympathetic ear. There had been moments during those first torturous months after Mitch's abduction that Alanna was not certain she could have survived without Elizabeth's steadfast support.

"Jonas is a good man, Alanna," Elizabeth told her gently.

"I know."

"And he'll make a good husband."

"I know."

"And from the way he enjoys all his nieces and nephews, it's obvious that he's marvelous father material."

After Mitch's abduction, she'd given up on the idea of ever having children. But this past year, whether because

of her growing feelings for Jonas, or because she was
turning thirty and her biological clock had picked up speed
or, even more likely, a combination of the two, Alanna
had begun to think more and more about being a mother.

Recently she'd begun spending her lunch hours at Wal-
ton Park, near her office in one of the four gleaming land-
mark high rises of the Embarcadero Center, watching the
children frolic. Only this morning, on her way to her office, she'd witnessed a young mother discreetly nursing her
infant. That poignantly maternal sight had been enough
to make Alanna's breasts ache all morning, as if in yearning.

"Mitch and I were going to have a baby," she said, closing her eyes against an unexpected stab of remorse. "He
always said that he wanted a quiet, wide-eyed little girl like
me. But I wanted a boy. A golden-haired, high-spirited
carbon copy of his father."

"If he was anything like Mitch, you would have turned
gray before your twenty-sixth birthday." Elizabeth patted
her expertly coiffed silver hair.

"And loved every minute of it," Alanna said on a rip-
pling sigh. Tears stung behind her lids. Reaching into her
black satin bag, she took out a tissue and dabbed at the
moisture below her eyes. "Gracious, I'm maudlin tonight. If I don't do something about my dreary attitude,
Jonas will decide he doesn't want to spend the rest of his
life with a weepy wife and stand me up at the altar."

"Never," Elizabeth predicted. "Jonas is not the kind of
man to turn tail and run the first time things get a little
rough, Alanna. He's a sticker. Watching his patience these
past nine months, while he coaxed you back into the world
of the living, it's clear he's signing on for the duration. For
better and worse."

"I know." Alanna forced a smile. "But that doesn't mean that I have to dump all the 'for worse' on him in the beginning. And what do you mean, he coaxed me back into the world of the living? It's not as if I've been a hermit.

"During these past five years I've given speeches all around the country, testified to the Senate Foreign Relations Committee, met with two presidents and three secretaries of state. And don't forget, I've also met with the president of France and had a private audience with the pope. And as if that weren't enough, I left my safe, predictable ivory tower of teaching to embark upon a highly visible new career."

Alanna's new career was due to Marian Burton-White, a chic, much-married, much-traveled woman in her fifties, who was also Alanna's paternal aunt and as different from her serious, attorney father as night from day. Having spent years as a successful free-lance photojournalist, supplying photos for an eclectic mix of publications, including *Life*, *The New York Times*, *Vanity Fair* and *Colliers*, she had—as she told the story—woken up one morning in a hut in Kenya, watched the dazzling orange sun rise over Mount Kilimanjaro, rubbed her back to soothe the vague aches that accompanied spending the past five nights sleeping on the ground and decided she was tired of living like a Gypsy.

Choosing publishing, she had established *San Francisco Trends* magazine and immediately offered her niece the job of special features editor. Believing the offer to be nothing more than kindhearted nepotism, Alanna had not taken her aunt's offer seriously. Until the following day, when Marian called her office at the University of San Francisco and asked her to lunch.

Over an excellent crab salad and a crisp, dry Napa Valley chardonnay, Marian had not only pointed out Alan-

na's sterling credentials for the job, but had made an offer
that proved she was perfectly serious. When Alanna
questioned the outrageous salary, her aunt had warned her
that were she to accept, she'd earn every penny.

Two weeks later, after a great deal of soul-searching,
Alanna had accepted. Marian's words proved prophetic.
Although the magazine articles she sought were nowhere
near as serious as the papers she was accustomed to as-
signing to her students, Alanna had never worked harder
in her life. Nor had she ever received such satisfaction from
her efforts. The past year had been both exhausting and
exhilarating.

"You've certainly come a long way from that young
woman who needed to take a Valium before she could talk
to strangers, or who threw up before every speech," Elizabeth agreed. "You've matured into an amazingly successful, self-assured woman. A virtual pillar of society. But
for all the men you allowed into your life, you might as
well have taken vows as a nun."

"In the beginning I thought Mitch would return."

"And later?"

"And later it was easier just to say no."

"Until Jonas."

"Yes." Elizabeth saw the soft light that shone in Alanna's eyes.

"Until Jonas." Alanna took a deep breath, garnering
courage to ask the question that had been worrying her all
evening. "Are you certain it doesn't bother you that I'm
remarrying?"

Elizabeth's answering gaze was solemn. "I've told you
innumerable times, dear, that all I've ever wanted for you
is your happiness. Which is why I went to considerable
trouble to fix you up with all those nice young men. Young
men you steadfastly refused to date. Besides getting past

emotional barricades that would have caused a lesser man to retreat, Jonas has made you happier than you've been in a very long time. And that, in turn, makes me very happy."

"He does make me happy," Alanna said. "Of course it's not a crazy, breathless kind of happy, like I had with Mitch. Being married to Mitch was like living on a roller coaster. Oh, there were lows—Mitch wasn't the easiest man to live with, he was impatient, reckless, and he had a temper that could blow you right off the face of the world—but just when I'd think we'd made a mistake, along would come a high." She smiled reminiscently. "Those wildly exhilarating highs were what always made me want to take another ride."

"And Jonas?" Elizabeth asked gently.

"Jonas is more like . . . I don't know exactly how to describe it, but being with Jonas is rather like sitting beside a quiet mountain stream in the summer sunshine, listening to the crystal water tumble over the rocks. Life's more peaceful. More tranquil." Immersed in thought, Alanna directed her gaze over the fog-shrouded Bay.

Her fiancé stood in the doorway, a blistering scowl on his features.

Peaceful. Tranquil. She made him sound boring. Worse than boring. Bland.

Dammit, Jonas Harte considered darkly, it hadn't been easy, treating Alanna Cantrell with kid gloves. From the moment he'd shown up at her door, ten minutes early for their appointment to discuss renovating her house, he'd known that his best friend's little sister was the woman he'd been waiting for all his life.

He knew the story of her husband's abduction. He also knew of Alanna's ill-fated efforts to gain his release. Even Mitchell Cantrell's death had not stopped her work on behalf of hostages. Determined that Americans would not forget those still being held in the Middle East, Alanna had become well-known and was much in demand as a public speaker.

But beneath the sleek, self-assured exterior, he'd sensed a vulnerability that had made him take things slowly, courting her with an almost old-world chivalry when what he wanted to do was drag her caveman style to the nearest bed and ravish her delectable body until they were too exhausted and too satiated to move.

They'd made love, of course. After all, this was the nineties, and they were both mature, sexual adults. But even in bed, at the moment of release, he'd found himself holding back, afraid his intense feelings for Alanna might scare her away before he got her to the altar.

So what had his uncharacteristic patience earned him? A woman who considered him tranquil. Safe. When what he wanted was to be Alanna's overwhelming passion. Dammit, he wanted her to be every bit as obsessed with him as he was with her.

Jonas swore softly, jamming his fists so deeply into his pockets that they tore. Change went spilling onto the carpet—two dimes, three pennies and a Canadian nickel he'd picked up somewhere. Jonas didn't care. He was too busy making plans, determined that the rest of Alanna Cantrell's evening would be anything but tranquil.

Tonight, the minute they were alone, he was going to take off the damned Sir Galahad mask and show Alanna exactly how passionate her seemingly bland fiancé could be.

And even more importantly, how passionate they could be together.

IT WAS MIDMORNING IN BEIRUT. The relentless sun burned its way through the smoke from the smoldering buildings. When the blindfold was taken from his eyes, Mitch blinked, allowing his pupils time to adjust to the brilliant light.

During these last three weeks the fighting had intensified, shells and missiles had screamed through the skies twenty-four hours a day. Ever since the escalation he'd been ensconced in an underground bunker. Forced to share the scant supplies, the single barrel of water, the cramped space, the lines between captor and captive had blurred. As they had intermittently over the last five years.

Mitch had spent the first four days of his captivity blindfolded, tied to a straight-backed, wooden chair, his hands lashed to the back legs. He'd been forbidden to speak, threatened with death if he uttered a single word.

Before the first week had passed, he had been stuffed into the trunk of a car and moved to the basement of an apartment building in suburban Beirut. There he'd spent the next six months, crammed into a tiny room with no light, forced to sleep on the floor, being beaten, kicked and tortured with taunts that his government—and worse yet, his family—had abandoned him.

Between beatings he'd been fed a meager diet of plain rice and tea. Weakened, he'd contracted pneumonia. Afraid that he would die before his political usefulness was exhausted, his captors had brought in a doctor, an internist at the prestigious American University Hospital and a sympathizer of the Islamic jihad. His near-fatal illness had had a positive outcome; he'd been given more nutritious meals, along with vitamins and food supplements. When the doctor prescribed daily doses of exercise and sunlight, Mitch could have kissed him.

Over the next several years he'd been shuttled from house to house, wrapped in packing tape like a mummy, crammed into car trunks and ambulances. Once he had even been stuffed into a too-short coffin. Each time he was taken away in the middle of the night, driven around the city in a purposefully convoluted manner in order to confuse his sense of direction. In most of the homes he'd been treated like a hated enemy, in a few as a barely tolerated houseguest. But in all of them he'd been closely guarded to ensure he would not escape.

During the second of his five years in captivity, he'd been held in a large, sprawling home in the hills with two other captives—a professor of biology at the university and a U.S. Embassy officer. Those days of companionship, while far from enjoyable, had made the following years of isolation even more difficult to bear.

Then, just when he'd thought that he was about to crack, he was moved again. For the past nine months he'd been confined at the home of Rafik Abdel Nammar. During those months the two men had developed a rapport, a form of mutual respect. Rafik had even admitted to a growing dissatisfaction with the idea of using American hostages as international bargaining chips. But his six brothers and numerous cousins and uncles belonged to the movement, and he was not one to turn his back on family. Nonetheless it was Rafik who had told Mitch last night that he was finally to be released as a goodwill gesture toward the West.

"So, soon you will be home," Rafik murmured as the two men stood in the middle of the Place des Canons, also known as the Place des Martyrs—the ruling Turks had hanged more than fifty people in the square during World War I. The few buildings that had not been reduced to rubble were bullet pocked. In walls where shells had struck, the wire innards of reinforced concrete were exposed and twisted. "What are your plans?"

"I'm going to take a long hot shower, drink a cold beer and make love to my wife." Five years! Sometimes it seemed like an eternity since he'd made love to Allie. At other times it seemed only yesterday.

Rafik's teeth flashed beneath his thick black mustache. "In that order?"

"Not exactly." Mitch returned his captor's smile with one that spoke of shared masculine fantasies. "The beer can wait."

He reached into his jeans pocket and pulled out a snapshot of Alanna, the only one he'd been allowed to keep. It had been taken one carefree afternoon at the beach shortly after she'd arrived in Lebanon to teach at the American University, a job Mitch knew she'd only taken in order to be with him. She was wearing a white bikini and smiling at the camera in a blatantly seductive way that made him marvel the lens hadn't melted. He couldn't count the number of times he'd looked at this picture. Touched it.

The paper was almost worn through. But Mitch didn't need a photograph; he could remember everything about his wife. It was as if her image had been burned onto his retina for all time, so that he could still close his eyes and see her smiling face, the love that had always shone so brightly in her soft green eyes. He took a deep breath, imagining that instead of the smoke and dust and garbage, he could smell her scent.

Rafik held out his hand. "Take care crossing the street, my friend. It would be a shame if you were to be hit by a bomb on your last day in Lebanon."

His last day. How many years had he waited for this moment? And now, when it had finally arrived, he felt strangely reluctant to leave. He remembered reading about the return of the Iranian hostages, how some of them had established ties with their captors. Stockholm Syndrome, it had been called. Refusing to fall prey to his own amateur psychology, Mitch forced himself to concentrate on the real reason for returning home: Allie.

He shook Rafik's outstretched hand. "I'd like to say I've enjoyed my visit, but that would be stretching the truth. Perhaps I'll simply say it's been interesting and leave it at that."

Rafik gave him a long, sober look. "You are the only newsman who knows us intimately," he said. "It is up to you to explain our cause to the world."

Mitch laughed, but the sound held no humor. "First I'd have to understand it myself." He shook his head, still awed by the madness that had turned an entire, sophisticated city—the sparkling gem of the Middle East—to rubble. Outside, in a dazzling setting of sea and mountains and valleys, through which had passed both prophets and armies, Lebanon lay drawn and quartered. The country was bleeding profusely; Mitch could only hope that both sides would learn to make accommodations before there was nothing left.

"*Mâalêsh*. Never mind," Rafik said. "It is enough that you will be honest." He smiled again. A smile that looked far more world-weary than his thirty-some years. "Good luck, Mitchell Cantrell. May you have a safe journey home."

"*Inshallâh,*" Mitch replied, murmuring the frequently cited expression that meant, Allah willing.

And now, if only Allah or some crazed, random sniper didn't interfere, in a few short hours he really would be back in the United States.

Back with Allie. His bride.

Mitch threw back his head and laughed. "Hot damn, I'm going home!" he shouted to everyone and no one. "Home!"

2

ALANNA TOOK ANOTHER SIP of champagne and tried to ignore the premonition of disaster that had been teasing at the back of her mind all day. It was only natural that she was feeling edgy, she assured herself. It wasn't as if she didn't have any stress in her life.

After all, how many people would be foolish enough to attempt to renovate a house the same year they began a new and demanding career? Not to mention planning a formal wedding? And if that weren't enough, the annual pestering from the various news organizations, printed and electronic, had begun. So far, she'd been able to keep news of her engagement from the press, but had spent the last two weeks holding her breath, waiting for the inevitable. During the past five years her public image had gradually shifted from grief-stricken bride and loyal wife to outspoken opponent of the government's foreign policy regarding hostages.

In a recent poll, *San Francisco Chronicle* readers had voted her one of ten women they most admired, right behind the First Lady. Instead of feeling flattered, Alanna found the increasing burden of public admiration suffocating.

She took another sip of champagne and wondered what the *Chronicle* subscribers would think when they discovered that not only was she making love to her architect, but was going to marry him in twenty-two, she took a glance at her watch, make that twenty-one short days.

"You look a million miles away," a deep voice murmured into her ear.

Alanna turned and smiled into Jonas's face. In no way did it resemble Mitch's classically handsome chiseled features, but her fiancé's harsh-hewn visage possessed a formidable strength of character that she'd found compelling from the moment they'd met.

His eyes betrayed cool intelligence and rigid determination, but the lines fanning outward from those coffee-dark depths revealed him to be a man who didn't scrimp on smiles. She especially liked his mouth. His lips were strong and firm and, for the entire nine months that she'd known him, Alanna had never seen them drawn in a disapproving line.

"I was thinking of all the things I still had to do before the wedding." All right, so it wasn't exactly the whole truth and nothing but the truth. A woman was entitled to some secrets from the man she was about to marry. Wasn't she?

"The offer to elope still stands."

The idea of running off to Lake Tahoe was becoming more enticing with each passing day. "No," Alanna said reluctantly. "Much as I'd love to forego the fanfare of a wedding, we have too many friends and family members who'd feel hurt if they were left out."

"It's your wedding, Alanna. Your day. You don't have to do anything you don't want to do."

"I know. But weddings are supposed to be a cause for celebration and, since we've already agreed to share the day, we should stick to our original plans."

Jonas shrugged his massive shoulders. Dressed in a dark navy suit with a thin burgundy stripe, he looked taller, stronger, more powerful than ever. "If you want to do it up big, it's fine with me. At least you don't have to worry about your passionate, lust-driven groom attacking you on the dance floor in front of all your friends at the reception."

He was looking down at her with a strangely challenging look that would have unnerved her if she hadn't known Jonas to be a remarkably easygoing man. "You've always been a perfect gentleman," she agreed.

"Perhaps that's my damn problem," he muttered.

Alanna frowned, certain that she must have misunderstood. "Excuse me?"

"Nothing," he said with his usual reassuring smile. Something indefinable flickered in his eyes, something that made her wonder why she'd never noticed how adept he was at concealing his thoughts. "I was just thinking out loud."

"Are you sure nothing's wrong?"

"Nothing I can't handle." He took the fluted glass out of her hand and placed it on the tray of a passing waiter. "And after politely listening to your aunt enumerate all the reasons why I'm a lucky bastard for having landed such a paragon of female perfection, without once interrupting to reveal a few of your more exceptional womanly talents, I feel I've earned a dance with my fiancée."

"I thought you'd never ask." Alanna went into his arms. Usually she felt safe and secure in his embrace, but when he wrapped his arms around her now, she tensed. There was something different about Jonas tonight. Something almost . . . dangerous.

But that was ridiculous, Alanna decided as she leaned against his solid strength and inhaled an indefinable male essence not due to any expensive after-shave or cologne, but was his alone. This was Jonas she was dancing with.

Safe, predictable Jonas.

It was Jonas's lips brushing her temple. Jonas's warm breath fanning her hair. Jonas's hands moving down her back, to the curve of her spine, cupping her buttocks, lifting her. . . .

"Jonas!" she gasped as he held her against an arousal he did not attempt to conceal. "What do you think you're doing?"

"Dancing with my fiancée," he said with a forced casualness that belied his throbbing groin.

Ever since overhearing Alanna's conversation with Elizabeth, he'd been thinking about what he was going to do to show her that he was not the boring, passionless man she'd apparently taken him to be. But his plan had backfired when his erotic thoughts billowed in his mind like smoke from a prairie fire; now, as he felt her body melding with his, Jonas found control difficult, to say the least.

What on earth had gotten into him tonight? Alanna wondered. When he caught the lobe of her ear between his teeth, she decided that this was the closest she'd ever come to making love in a vertical position. Even as she told herself that she should back away from a potentially embarrassing situation, she couldn't resist the swelling virility between Jonas's legs.

"How much champagne have you had?"

"Only half a glass. I don't need alcohol when I'm around you, Alanna. You're intoxicating enough all by yourself." He bent his head and brushed his lips against hers. The brief kiss was like a flare of sparklers against her skin. "Just looking at you, touching you, can make me drunker than a magnum of champagne. A flagon of robust port."

"Gracious!" Her sexual senses were suddenly vividly alive, heightened even further as her body strained against him. "I hadn't realized you could be so poetic."

"I had an excellent muse. . . . Do you have any idea how much I want you?" he asked, burying his face in the curve of her neck, drinking in her scent. The complex, mysterious fragrance of her perfume made him think of smoldering heat, steamy sex. It made him want to drag her off and make love to her in a dark, moist forest.

When his tongue touched her warming flesh, tremors of excitement surged through her. She never would have expected this edgy passion. Not from Jonas. Even as her head spun, Alanna found herself wanting to explore this surprising phenomenon further.

"I think I have a pretty good idea." She reached up and traced his lips with a peach-tinted fingernail. Why had she never noticed how sensual his mouth was? He caught her hand and turned it, pressing his lips against the fragrant skin at the inside of her wrist. Her pulse jumped.

"Too bad we're not alone." The banked fire in his normally calm eyes stirred Alanna more than she ever would have thought possible. It echoed her own feelings. It unleashed desires she had safely locked away—passions she thought she'd never feel again.

"You know," she murmured, "now that you mention it, I believe I feel a headache coming on."

He arched a dark brow. "Really?"

"It feels like a migraine," she said. "At least." Was that soft breathless voice really hers? "I think perhaps I should go home." Their eyes met. Shared desire thickened the air around them until even breathing was an effort.

"To bed," Jonas said.

She was so shaky. The room, the city, the entire world was suddenly unbelievably shaky. If San Francisco wasn't experiencing an earthquake, she was in serious trouble.

Going up onto her toes, she touched her lips to his. "To bed."

"I'M NOT A HERO."

Mitch sprawled back in the gilt chair and stretched his

Mitch sprawled back in the gilt chair and stretched his long legs in front of him. After a whirlwind twelve hours, he was safely ensconced in the U.S. Air Force Base at Wiesbaden, waiting to be interviewed by intelligence officials before his return to the States.

He glared down at his feet, which were aching in an unaccustomed pair of shoes. Black wing tips, no less. His comfortably broken-in cordovan loafers had been taken away from him the first night of his captivity and he'd been kept shoeless to prevent him from trying to escape. As much as he wanted to take them off, or at least loosen the black laces, Mitch reluctantly decided that sore feet were a small price to pay for his return to civilization.

"Try telling that to the American public," Daniel S. Buckner, the CIA bureau chief, said dryly. "They want a hero, Cantrell. Looks as if you're elected."

"What's that quote about 'Unhappy is the land that needs heroes'?" Mitch countered. "Look, I'm willing to tell you everything I know, which isn't a hell of a lot. But then I just want to get back to my own life. With my wife. Who I still haven't been allowed to call."

The older man shrugged off Mitch's pointed complaint. "We don't want the word getting out about your release until we've debriefed you. This place will be overrun with reporters soon enough."

He took a pack of cigarettes out of his pocket and offered the pack to Mitch, who refused. Buckner lighted one for himself, leaned back and eyed Mitch through a cloud of blue smoke. "So," he said, "let's start with the day you were abducted."

Mitch exhaled an exasperated breath. If they were going to go through the last five years one day at a time, he'd be a grizzled old man before he got home to Allie.

"It was our anniversary," he began, not bothering to conceal his escalating irritation. "And we were on our way to dinner."

"Where?"

"The Commodore." The hell with etiquette. Mitch kicked off his shoes. It was looking to be a very long night.

THE SHORT DRIVE to Alanna's home seemed to take an eternity.

"Finally," Jonas said with relief. Pulling off his burgundy tie, he tossed it carelessly over the curved ivory-inlaid arms of the papier-mâché chair in the foyer. Alanna had discovered the chair at an estate sale in Mendocino last month. It was more than her budget allowed, and he'd enjoyed buying it for her as an engagement present. "I thought we'd never get out of there."

"You certainly seemed in a hurry." Alanna shrugged out of her black cashmere coat. Although the days were warming up, the San Francisco nights were still cool. She'd gotten chilled on the walk in from the car, but one look at the smoldering flames in Jonas's dark eyes was enough to warm her to the core.

"About some things." He took her coat and hung it on the brass-and-ivory hall tree. Desire hammered at him. Jonas forced it down. For now. "But there are certain things I prefer to do very, very slowly."

He definitely was different tonight. Alanna studied Jonas surreptitiously from beneath her lowered lashes. He'd always possessed an aura of steely strength; it was one of the things that had attracted her to him. But tempering the strength had always been a gentleness that had allowed her to let down her defenses for long enough to fall in love with him.

But tonight . . . tonight Jonas radiated a masculinity so powerful that it threatened to overwhelm her. When a slow alien warmth began to seep through her veins, she trembled.

"Cold?" he asked.

"No," she whispered. His steady, brown eyes were looking at her. Looking hard. Looking deep. His intent gaze both unnerved and excited her. "I think I'm burning up."

His smile was slow, sensual and extremely dangerous. "And just think, the night's still young." Before she could perceive his intention, he'd scooped her into his arms and was carrying her effortlessly up the spiral staircase.

"Jonas! What are you doing?"

"What do you think?" he inquired, entering the bedroom at the top of the stairs. He set her on her feet beside the lacy white iron bed, then moved around the room lighting fragrant white candles. "I'm seducing my fiancée."

He stopped for a moment beside her closet door, where her wedding dress hung—an uncharacteristic froth of ivory lace, adorned with seed pearls. At first she'd resisted dressing up like a traditional virginal bride; she had, after all, been married before. But Elizabeth had insisted that since she and Mitch had eloped the first time around, Alanna was entitled to live out her childhood fantasy of a formal wedding. And although she'd remained doubtful, one look into the dressing-room mirror last week had changed Alanna's mind. She looked, she'd thought in amazement, almost beautiful.

Jonas toyed with the diaphanous ivory veil. "Promise me something?"

"What?"

"That on our wedding night you'll wear nothing but your wedding ring, your pearls and this veil."

The scene he'd sketched flashed into her mind, so vividly erotic that it made her knees shake. "Yes," she managed in a soft tremulous tone.

He returned to stand in front of her, so close that Alanna could no longer tell if it was her heart beating so rapidly or his. "I love you, Alanna." His hands skimmed over her bare shoulders and down her arms, his touch as light as the rain that had begun to fall outside the window. "Let me show you how much."

"Oh, yes." A breath she hadn't even been aware of holding escaped unevenly. She heard the sound of a zipper being lowered. A moment later the green silk bodice of her dress fell to her waist. With a smooth, easy gesture, he tugged down the strapless satin camisole, as well.

His dark gaze roved over her bared breasts. His eyes were hot. Hungry. Submitting to his supremely masculine appraisal, Alanna felt deliciously illicit. "Have I ever told you that I love your skin?" he asked.

"It doesn't tan. Never. Not even in..." Her voice drifted off when she realized she'd been about to mention Beirut. Although Jonas had encouraged her to talk about those days, about her marriage to Mitch, the subject had always remained off-limits in the bedroom.

Jonas watched the flash of pained memory in her eyes but did not comment on it. "Tans are highly overrated. They give you freckles." His fingers glided over her, leaving a trail of sparks on her warming flesh. "Not to mention premature wrinkles. My aunt Kathleen, who you'll meet at the wedding, has played golf every day of her adult life. The woman's only fifty but she looks like an advertisement for a tannery. Your creamy flesh, on the other hand, has always reminded me of porcelain."

He bent his head and dropped a kiss against a budding nipple. The muscles of her stomach contracted. "I take that back," he murmured as his lips moved to the other breast, treating it to a torture just as sweet, just as prolonged. "Porcelain is too hard. Too cold. Your skin is like satin." When his tongue stroked a long, wet swath across the aching fullness of her breasts, a strangled sound of pleasure escaped her parted lips. "Warm, liquid satin."

"Jonas—" She pressed her hands against his chest. She needed time. Time to think. Time to comprehend what he was doing to her.

Jonas looked down into her exquisite face. Her wide green eyes were dark and dazed. "Want me to stop?"

"Yes. For just a minute. Until I catch my breath." Her fingers, belying her words, fumbled with the buttons of his dress shirt. "I take that back. Don't stop." She couldn't remember ever wanting—no, needing—a man as much as she did Jonas at this moment. "I don't know. Everything's suddenly so different. So confusing."

When she would have looked away, Jonas gathered her hair in his hand, tilting her head back, so her eyes were forced to meet his again. "May I make a suggestion?"

She hesitated. "What?"

His fingers glided down her throat, over her collarbone, her breasts, her rib cage, roaming seductively down to her stomach. "Why don't you just relax and go with the flow?"

With the twenty-twenty vision of hindsight, Alanna had come to realize that she had been incredibly naive when she married Mitch. Intent on changing things, vowing never to be a victim again, never to be weak again, she'd taken control of her life with a gritty determination that others had described as nothing less than an obsession. She had not allowed their warnings to deter her in her goal of becoming strong. Confident. Competent.

She knew she was no longer the sweet, acquiescent young bride who had watched her adored husband thrown into the back of a car in Beirut. And even if she wanted to, which she didn't, Alanna knew that she could never be that woman again.

But tonight things were somehow different.

When she would have answered Jonas, when she would have agreed to anything, his mouth fastened onto hers. The kiss sent her reeling. Her hands moved to his shoulders, grasping him, as if to keep from tumbling off the edge of a rapidly spinning world.

It didn't help. She felt herself falling, effortlessly, like a feather caught in a warm spiral of summer breeze, until the crisp flower-sprigged sheets were beneath her back. Reason disintegrated and there were no more thoughts. Only sensations. Feelings. Heat.

She surrendered to him mindlessly, willing to go wherever he took her. Alanna didn't question how clothes were whisked from her. She only knew that piece by piece they disappeared, as if by magic.

Jonas's hands touched, stroked, aroused. His mouth coaxed, tempted, beguiled. She was boneless, pliant before his increasing ruthlessness. Her skin was hot and smooth and damp under his hands. His lips loitered at her breast and she arched her back, thrusting her fingers through his hair. But he was like quicksilver, teasing, tempting, never staying in one place long enough to satisfy.

When his tongue dived wetly into her navel, she uttered a muffled cry. When his teeth nibbled at the flaming skin on the inside of her thigh, she called out his name. His warm breath teased her. His tongue brought her to the brink of a precipice, but before she could go over the edge, he retreated, leaving her weak and shuddering.

This was how he'd wanted her. Dazed with passion, flushed with pleasure. On the edge of reason himself, Jonas lifted himself. Gazing down at her, he felt like a pagan conqueror, intent upon claiming new territory.

He understood that she'd never forget her husband, had known that from the beginning. And he'd accepted it. But he intended to expunge for all time any memories Alanna possessed of Mitchell Cantrell in her bed. He wanted to scorch away the lingering touch of Cantrell's hands, any tastes, sensations or feelings from his lips. He wanted to claim Alanna for his own. Not only her body. All of her—mind and heart and soul.

"Tell me," he said, drinking in a huge draught of air so that he could speak. "Tell me what you want."

Later, when her mind had cleared and her blood had cooled, Alanna would realize that there were levels of intimacy. The one she was entering upon with Jonas tonight was stronger, more binding than any she'd ever experienced before.

At this moment, all she knew was that if she couldn't have him soon—now—she would surely die.

"You. I want you."

Nothing had prepared her for the sudden violence of need that erupted inside her. She had thought she'd known passion. Believed that she'd experienced desire. But she'd been wrong. No one had ever given her so much. No one had ever taken so much from her.

With a strength she hadn't known she possessed, she was pulling his clothes from him, her desperate hands fretting over his flesh, fanning flames he'd managed to keep carefully banked. Until now. "I want all of you. Inside of me."

The ripe scent of passion filled the air, mingling with the sweet vanilla of the candles and the fragrance of the rain. The sheets became hot and twisted as they rolled over the bed, mouth to mouth, flesh to flesh. Their skin was slick and hot. Her breath rushed from between her lips into his mouth. Her body craved. His burned. Wherever his hands lingered, she ached. Wherever her lips loitered, he flamed.

Heat poured out of her and into him. No longer pliant, she grew strong. Agile. Her arms and legs wrapped around him, enveloping him like warm silk, drawing him in.

"I love you." They spoke together.

He wanted to watch her face, to see the passion in her eyes as he took her over the edge, but his own vision was clouded. He plunged into her, his long strokes driving her deeper and deeper into the mattress. A heavy pressure was building up at the base of his spine and just when Jonas thought he couldn't hold back another moment, her eyes flew open and she uttered a sudden cry of pleasure.

Viewing the amazement in their swirling green depths, Jonas experienced a heady burst of pure masculine satisfaction that she had experienced the excitement he had wanted her to know. Then, covering her trembling lips with his, he gave in to the explosive needs of his own body.

THEY LAY IN A TANGLE of arms and legs. Naked, shaken and content. The candles had burned down; the rain continued to stream down the window and drum softly on the roof. The room had grown cool. Both Jonas and Alanna felt too lazily complacent to search for the wedding-ring quilt that had slid onto the floor.

"I feel absolutely decadent," she said when she could speak again.

He ran his hand down her side from shoulder to thigh. "Decadent and delectable."

How could so light a touch send desire shimmering through her again so soon? "I have a confession to make," Alanna said quietly.

"Oh?" He turned his head, looking down into her flushed face. Pleasure glowed in her eyes. But there was confusion there, as well.

"I think I may have underestimated you."

"In what way?"

She trailed her fingernail down his chest. His cooling skin was still damp, redolent with the scent of their love-making. "It's difficult to explain." Unable to resist, she pressed her lips against his flesh. "I don't want you to misunderstand."

Because of his inadvertent eavesdropping, he understood only too well. Deciding there was no point in making her say out loud what her body had professed so eloquently, he bent his head and pressed a gentle kiss against her temple. "Don't worry about explaining anything. Unless you're trying to delicately break the news that you're calling off the wedding."

"Are you kidding?" She laughed, a throaty, sexy laugh that Jonas had never heard before. "You are the man every woman's been looking for... intelligent, a sense of humor, a good career. You are also incredibly gentle and kind and considerate—"

"You're making me sound like a Boy Scout," he complained.

She kissed him. A long, delicate kiss that made him want her again. She made him feel eighteen. A horny eighteen.

"I'm not finished. You are also unbelievably sexy." She shook her head in mild amazement. "Talk about your still waters. Who would have guessed that beneath that calm, steady exterior beat the heart of a wild man?"

"I think I like that better than the Boy Scout stuff."

"But don't you see?" Alanna said earnestly. "It's exactly that unbelievable combination of stability and uncivilized passion that makes you such a catch. You're every woman's dream, Jonas Benjamin Harte.... In fact, now that I think about it, you could even be Prince Charming in the flesh."

"Remind me to send my armor out to be shined before our wedding."

Laughing, Alanna lifted her hand to his chest. Her sparkling eyes took a long, leisurely look at his nude body, sprawled magnificently amidst the tangled sheets of her bed. "Don't bother," she said, flinging herself atop him. "I think I prefer you this way."

He stroked her hair. "I'll never wear clothes again."

"Never? Won't that get a little chilly in San Francisco?"

His smiling lips nibbled at hers. "Ah, but I'll have my sexy wife to keep me warm."

The phone rang. They ignored it. Jonas's hands caressed her back, his fingers trailing little tongues of flame up and down the delicate bones of her spine.

The phone continued to ring.

"Maybe I should see who it is," Alanna murmured.

"They'll go away." When he took her bottom lip between his teeth and tugged, she felt a corresponding pull between her legs.

And still the phone rang.

"Damn. I'm sorry." She grabbed the receiver from the ebony bedside table. "But I've never been able to resist a ringing telephone." She didn't add that such behavior had developed in those early days when she waited impotently by a frustratingly silent phone for word of Mitch.

"Just get rid of whoever it is, fast." Jonas brushed her hair out of the way to allow his lips access to her neck. "In the interest of fair play, I've decided to let you have your wicked way with me."

"You're on," she agreed instantly. "Hello?" For an extended moment, all Alanna could hear was the unmistakable hiss of long-distance wires. "Is anyone there?"

"It's probably a wrong number," Jonas said, shifting onto his side in order to settle her more comfortably against him. "Hang up."

"But it's long distance."

"Hello?" A deep voice finally came on the line.

"Hello?" Alanna repeated as Jonas's seductive hands cupped her breasts. "Who is this?"

"Allie?"

Jonas felt the change in her instantly. Her flesh, warm and fluid, turned to ice. "Oh, my God . . . Mitch?" It was a ragged whisper, easily heard in the sudden stillness of the bedroom, but indiscernible over the miles.

"Allie?" Mitch repeated with a shout, as if the effort would make her words ring clearer at his end of the phone. "It's me, Allie. Mitch. Your ever-lovin' husband. The bastards finally let me go, sweetheart. I'm coming home!"

3

IT HAD TO BE a practical joke, Alanna told herself. Some sick prankster's idea of fun. Mitch was dead. The clandestine CIA operatives in Syria and Jordan had said so. The State Department had confirmed it. And if you couldn't believe the United States government, whom could you believe?

"My husband is dead," she stated. Both her hands and her voice were shaking badly. "And if you ever dare call me again, I'll file a complaint with the police. And the telephone company. And the entire U.S. government. With the president, himself, if necessary."

"Allie, sweetheart, it really is me," Mitch insisted. "To quote Mark Twain, the reports of my death have been greatly exaggerated."

Jonas hitched himself up to a sitting position and watched Alanna carefully. She was as pale as a ghost and in her eyes he could see a mingling of fierce pain and reluctant hope. "It can't be you. It's impossible."

"Allie, how many times have you heard me say that the difficult I can pull off immediately, but the impossible takes a little longer?"

No. It couldn't be. "Mitch?" Alanna asked, immersed in her own turbulent thoughts.

"It really is me, honeybun. In person," he confirmed cheerfully.

Something deep inside Alanna told her that it was true. Somehow Mitch had escaped. It really was him on the other end of the long-distance line. But common sense continued to insist that it was impossible. On the outside chance that it really was her husband, she hated to ask the next question. But she'd received so many crank calls over the years that she couldn't accept his words at face value.

"Tell me something about us," she insisted. "Something the press wouldn't have known."

Mitch wondered when his sweet, acquiescent Alanna had become so distrusting, then decided the answer was obvious. When her husband had been kidnapped. "I brought you tulips." The memory took no effort; the mental picture of her holding the colorful flowers and looking like springtime had kept him sane. "Pier Uttenbos brought them back from Holland."

"That was in the *Los Angeles Herald Examiner*," she said. Every story, every paragraph, every word written about Mitch's abduction had been seared onto her mind for all time.

Frustrated, Mitch tried again. "You'd lectured that day on Thucydides, but when I tried to show off my expertise, you insisted that you didn't want to talk about Greek historians, or the war, or even the network."

Hope was a hummingbird, fluttering its wings inside her, but there'd been so many false alarms. "*People Magazine*," she said. She had never known where they'd obtained such personal information, but there it had been, right beside the picture of Mitch and herself on their honeymoon.

"Dammit, Allie!" *No*, Mitch reminded himself. *Calm down*. He hadn't waited all this time, hadn't survived against insurmountable odds only to yell at her. "Okay," he said with a long-suffering sigh. "Let's try this. You told me that years from now, when we were both old and gray and sitting on our front porch watching our grandchildren playing tag in the flower beds, you wanted to look back and remember our anniversary as a special, magical time."

"Oh, my God!" Alanna pressed her palm against her chest, to see if her heart was still beating. "It is you. Where are you?"

The line crackled, the tenuous overseas connection threatened to break up. "Allie, sweetheart, I can't hear you.... Damn this phone system," he complained in a flare of temper. "Look, honey, I'm going to have to make this fast, before we lose the connection completely. They're putting me on an air force jet tonight. I'll be at the Mayflower Hotel in D.C. tomorrow. Meet me there, okay? I've had nothing to do for the past five years but plan that anniversary celebration we were so rudely cheated out of."

"But, Mitch—" Before she could finish, the phone went dead in her hand. She stared down at it.

Jonas could no longer keep quiet. "Alanna." His hands cupped her chin, lifting her downcast gaze to his. She was trembling, and her unfocused eyes were dark and glazed. "Alanna," he repeated, shaking her gently. "Who was it?"

Alanna felt as if she were drowning. Struggling for air, she took several deep breaths. "It was Mitch," she managed.

"Are you sure?"

"P-p-positive," she stammered. "Oh, G-God, Jonas, he knew. Knew about the grandchildren." Her throat was closing up; she took another long draught of air. "And the g-g-garden."

She was cold. Damn cold. "Let me get you a drink. Some brandy."

"No." When she shook her head, her chestnut hair skimmed her ashen cheeks. "I have to..." Her voice faded as she looked blindly around the room. "He wanted me to meet . . . I have to pack. . . . To go. . . ."

This was a nightmare, Jonas assured himself. After making love to Alanna, he'd fallen asleep. All he needed to do was make a concerted effort and he'd wake up. He blinked. Once, twice, three times. Then pinched himself for good measure. When nothing happened, when things remained exactly as they were, his heart took a plunge.

"Go where?" He prided himself on his ability to keep his voice strong. Controlled. "Where was he calling from?"

Alanna stared at Jonas, as if she couldn't quite conceive who he was. And what he was doing here, in her bed. "I don't know."

"Then how do you know where you're going?" he asked gently, worried by the way color still hadn't returned to her cheeks.

Good question, Alanna conceded. *Trust Jonas to remain unwaveringly practical in the midst of a hurricane.* He was always so calm; that was one of the reasons she'd fallen in love with him. That was one of the reasons she'd agreed to marry him.

"He'll be in Washington tomorrow." Her voice was steadier now, but the quietly spoken words barely made it past her lips. "He said something about an air force jet."

"This is awfully off-the-wall," he insisted. "Let me call someone for you. Someone who can check this out."

She pressed her lips together, struggling for restraint. "I'll call."

For some reason she could not fully understand, Alanna wanted to be alone when she talked with Kyle Fields, the State Department liaison to the hostage families. Although she knew it was ridiculous, talking to Kyle about Mitch while she was lying naked in bed with Jonas would make her feel like an adulteress. Getting out of bed on legs that only wobbled slightly, she slipped into the ivory silk robe Jonas had given her for her birthday last month.

"Jonas." She turned. "Would you do something for me?"

"Anything."

"Would you please go downstairs and make us some coffee? This could turn out to be a very long night."

Her refusal to accept his comfort stung, but Jonas kept his feelings to himself. "Sure." He went to the closet and pulled out a pair of well-worn jeans. Although he and Alanna weren't technically living together, over the past months he'd begun keeping a few changes of clothes at her house, while she'd moved a few things onto his boat. "Want me to bring it up to you when it's done?"

"I think I'd rather come down."

The movement of his shoulders was forced, but he managed to make it noncommittal. "Suit yourself." He turned in the doorway. When he saw Alanna slumped in the wing chair like a broken doll, his heart went out to her. "Alanna." He allowed her name to linger on the air for a long, suspended moment. "If you need anything—anything at all—just yell."

"I'll be fine," she insisted, in a voice she wished were stronger. "Jonas?"

It was barely a whisper, but easily heard in the stillness of the room. She suddenly looked so small, so alone, that Jonas had to jam his hands into his back pockets to keep from reaching out and pulling her into his arms. "Yeah?"

Traitorous tears glistened wetly in her eyes, belying her wobbly attempt at a smile. "Thank you. For everything."

His own smile was no more successful. "Anytime."

Alanna watched him leave; she listened to his footfalls on the stairs, the sound of water running in the kitchen. Then, taking a deep breath, she dialed the number she knew by heart.

JONAS WAS GOING stark raving mad. She'd been on the phone for more than thirty minutes. How long did it take to confirm whether or not the call was a hoax? Whether her husband was alive or dead? *Former husband*, he corrected firmly. Alanna's brief marriage to Mitch Cantrell had come to an end with the State Department's official declaration of the newsman's murder, three years ago.

It wasn't Cantrell, Jonas assured himself. This was just another sick prank. In three short weeks Alanna was going to be his. All his. Forever.

Then he recalled that slender light of hope shining in her eyes, when she'd thought Mitch might actually be the one calling, and felt a jolt of something resembling jealousy. What the hell kind of man was he to be jealous of a ghost?

He was about to go upstairs and find out for himself what was going on when she suddenly appeared in the kitchen, looking even more stunned, if possible, than she had when he'd left her.

"It's true." She answered the question she saw in his dark eyes. "Mitch is alive."

Jonas waited to gauge his reaction. When no immediate rush of feelings came, he decided that he must be as numb as Alanna looked. "I see." He poured her a cup of the coffee she'd requested earlier. Had it only been a half hour? he wondered as he added the sugar and cream he knew she favored. It seemed like an eon.

They were standing at opposite ends of the room. A thick, heavy silence settled over them. Alanna felt herself tensing as it dragged on. "I don't think that's such a good idea," she said finally when she saw him pour a generous splash of brandy into her cup.

"You were out of decaf." He crossed the room, cup in hand. "The brandy should negate the effects of the caffeine. Besides, you still look as if you've just seen a ghost."

"Now that's a pithy analysis." Alanna accepted the cup he held out to her. When their fingers brushed, she felt a lingering warmth she'd thought they'd left upstairs in the now cold bed. "I suppose, in a manner of speaking, I have."

She sank onto a kitchen chair and wrapped her fingers tightly around the cup. She took a sip, unsurprised to find it strong and steaming. Perfect. Everything Jonas did, he did carefully, perfectly. She'd witnessed him measure a two-by-four three times before making the cut, had watched him paint windowsills with a concentration that was almost otherworldly. As for the flowered wallpaper in the foyer, she defied anyone to locate the seams.

"Want to talk about it?"

The brandy was working its way through her veins, warming her blood, soothing the painful pounding in her chest. "I don't know what to say," she told him honestly.

Squatting beside her, he stroked a thumb down her cheek. "Perhaps you ought to begin with where Mitch was calling from." Jonas prided himself on his ability to say his rival's name without choking on it. "I take it he wasn't in Lebanon."

"No." Alanna drew a deep breath. "He called from Germany. I still don't understand all the logistics, but somehow, after he was released he managed to make it to the embassy. They got him out of the country and to Germany two days ago."

"Two days?" Jonas asked unbelievingly. "It took two days to notify you?"

"Apparently they needed the time to debrief him."

Even as he dreaded the idea of losing Alanna to her resurrected husband, Jonas was angry at the bureaucratic thinking that had kept her from learning the truth immediately. "That stinks."

She took another soothing sip of the brandy-laced coffee. "That's what I said." Because her throat was suddenly dry she swallowed. Once. Twice. Three times. "The State Department managed to link me up with Wiesbaden," she murmured. "This time Mitch and I were able to talk for five whole minutes before we were cut off."

"How did he sound?"

"Tired. Excited. Fed up with diplomatic policy and bureaucratic rules." She managed a weak smile. "Mitch never was much for rules. I couldn't count the times he ignored curfews or drove into territories the government had declared off-limits to journalists. He drove the network executives up a wall with his devil-may-care stunts."

"I can imagine," Jonas said quietly, watching the memory gleam in her eyes.

"They were always threatening to assign him back to the States. But of course they never did."

"And they wouldn't have," Jonas guessed. "Not so long as he kept sending back those dynamite pictures."

This time the smile was a little stronger. "That's what Mitch always said." She folded her hands and tried to remain calm as she broached the next uncomfortable subject. "I couldn't tell him about you. About us," she amended softly. "Not on the phone. It would have been too cruel."

"I agree." Jonas knew that Alanna loved him. He also knew from long intimate conversations with her over the past nine months that she was no longer the young naive wife Mitchell Cantrell had married. And although Jonas was honestly sorry about all Mitch had been through, he believed that Alanna now belonged with him. "So, what happens now?" Jonas's eyes met hers, looking deep.

Unable to meet his probing gaze, Alanna looked off into the middle distance, remembering how she'd felt when she and Jonas had been making love. It had been exhilarating. Stunning. And it had felt so very, very right.

"I have to go to Washington first thing in the morning. There's going to be some kind of ceremony in the White House Rose Garden. I called Elizabeth. The poor woman sounded as stunned as I feel. Of course, she'll be coming with me."

"Of course," he agreed, wondering exactly how enthusiastic Elizabeth Cantrell would continue to be about his and Alanna's upcoming nuptials, now that her son was back in the picture. He stood up and crossed the kitchen to where Alanna kept the telephone book, in a drawer at the end of the ceramic counter. "I'll call and get our tickets."

"That would be nice," Alanna said absently, remembering how Elizabeth had begun to sob when she was told of her son's release. She had never heard her mother-in-law cry before. Not even at Mitch's memorial service. "I don't think I could deal with times and flight numbers right now." Jonas's words suddenly sank in. "Did you say *our* tickets?"

He was leafing through the Yellow Pages. "Of course."

She stared at him. "Jonas, you can't come with me."

"Why not?"

"Because we don't even know if Mitch understands that he and I are no longer married. I certainly can't welcome him back from five long years of terrorist captivity with a fiancé by my side!"

"I'm not insensitive, Alanna. Of course I won't be standing by your side in the Rose Garden, while the president pins a medal on your former husband. But if you think I'm going to let you go through something like this alone, you're dead wrong."

She stood up, her eyes passionate as she began to pace the kitchen floor. "You don't understand, it's too great a risk. The press is bound to see us together."

"I'll simply make sure they don't."

She spun around, her hands balled into fists in the pockets of her robe. "It's too risky."

"Trust me."

How many times had she heard that? Alanna wondered. The first time he'd assured her that she'd love the solarium he wanted to build off her kitchen. Needless to say, he'd been right. It was her favorite room in the house. The second time had been when he'd first made love to her, soothing her fears and banishing the lingering feeling that by going to bed with Jonas she was cheating on her husband. The third time was when he convinced her that a future together was worlds more fulfilling than any life— no matter how successful—they might forge individually.

"You know I do," she whispered, her trust—and her love—shining in her eyes.

Yes. He knew that. But he also knew that she'd once trusted—and loved—Mitch Cantrell. Wishing he could whisk her away to some remote, tropical island, where the State Department could never find them, Jonas forced an encouraging smile.

"Jonas?" The events of the past hour were crowding in upon Alanna. So many emotions. So many memories. "Could you do something for me?"

"Anything," he affirmed yet again. Giving up on his search for the airline's telephone number, Jonas crossed the room and took her gently by the shoulders. She was weeping and unaware of it.

"Would you just hold me?"

His arms wrapped around her. "It's going to be all right, Alanna," he insisted, his lips pressed against her hair. "We're going to be all right."

AFTER A SLEEPLESS NIGHT, they picked up Elizabeth at six o'clock. Wanting to give them some much-needed time alone, Jonas waited in the taxi, while Alanna went into her mother-in-law's house. Ten minutes later they came out. From the tight set of her lips when she observed him in the back seat, Jonas realized that Elizabeth had been fore-warned. From the strained expression on Alanna's features, Jonas suspected that Elizabeth's response to the news that he would be accompanying them to the capital was less than enthusiastic.

"Hello, Jonas," Elizabeth greeted him with forced po-liteness as she claimed the front seat next to the driver.

Jonas was not surprised her tone lacked its usual warmth. He'd already suspected that Elizabeth would have her own agenda for this Washington trip. Sensing the pain she must have suffered these past five years, he wasn't about to enter into a battle for Alanna's love. At least, not until he determined that war had been declared.

"Good morning," he said. "You look well."

She managed a smile at that. "Always the gentleman, aren't you, Jonas? As a matter of fact, I look like hell."

"Of course you don't," Alanna insisted loyally as she joined Jonas in the back of the cab. "You look lovely."

"The two of you are liars," Elizabeth retorted. "Charm-ing ones, but liars, just the same. At my age, lack of sleep leaves me looking as if I've been run over by a bulldozer." She pulled out a gold compact, scowling at her reflection. "Mitch will think his mother's turned into an old crone while he's been away." When her voice cracked, she closed the compact with a decided snap and turned away, pretending a sudden interest in the scenery flashing by the passenger window.

"He'll think you're beautiful," Jonas insisted. "All sons believe their mothers are the most beautiful women in the world."

"Flatterer."

"Not a flatterer, but a son. And I know damn well that Mitch Cantrell loves his mother every bit as much as I love mine."

Elizabeth bit her lip as she turned in her seat to look at him. Her eyes held reluctant admiration. "You're a good man, Jonas Harte. When I first met you, all I could think was how lucky Alanna was to have you in her life."

He had to ask. "And now?"

She looked directly at him. "I love my son, Jonas."

"As well you should."

"I want him to be happy."

"Elizabeth." Alanna simply had to speak. "I don't think this is the time or the place—"

"On the contrary, dear," Elizabeth retorted, her voice edged with that innate steely strength Alanna had witnessed during those long agonizing months when there had been no word of Mitch. "I believe it's imperative that we all understand that Mitch has gone through a terrible ordeal. If he were to learn that along with five years of freedom, he's also lost his wife, it could prove devastating."

It was emotional blackmail, pure and simple. But nothing that Alanna hadn't been telling herself, these past hours. "You don't have to worry, Elizabeth," she assured her mother-in-law. "Jonas and I intend to be discreet. But I have to tell Mitch that our marriage was dissolved when he was declared dead. Otherwise he'll find out from the press, which would be much more painful."

"On that, at least, we agree," Elizabeth said.

They rode the remainder of the way to the airport in silence. Jonas covered Alanna's hand with his and from time to time he squeezed her fingers reassuringly. Although Alanna knew she was going to need all the emotional support she could get, she couldn't help wondering if Jonas was being entirely honest with her when he promised to stay on the sidelines.

He'd been so incredibly different last night. So intense. She couldn't shake the uneasy feeling that he was motivated by something more basic than merely offering support. Such as a masculine need to stake a claim.

But that was ridiculous, she assured herself. Just because Jonas had displayed an uncharacteristic, passionate side in bed, it didn't necessarily mean he was going to pull a Dr. Jekyll and Mr. Hyde and turn into an entirely different person.

Did it?

Whenever she glanced up at him, his brown eyes were warm and reassuring. But there was something else swirling in those coffee-brown depths. Something Alanna could not quite discern. Something that was making her increasingly uneasy.

The trip to Washington was decidedly uncomfortable. Alanna and Jonas sat on one side of the first-class aisle, Elizabeth on the other. There was scant conversation as each remained lost in thought about Mitch's miraculous return from the dead.

And what such a resurrection was going to mean to their lives.

4

IF MITCH THOUGHT that the past five years had been difficult, waiting for Allie to arrive was proving next to impossible.

"I still don't see why I have to hang around here," he complained to Alex Haynes, the State Department officer who'd arranged for the suite at the Mayflower Hotel. "Why can't I meet Allie at the airport?"

"You know National is always crawling with press," Haynes argued. "And your face is too well-known."

"Do you guys realize that it's been five years since I've seen my wife?" Mitch demanded. "When I called her, I pictured myself standing at the end of the jetway with flowers in my hand."

During Mitch's entire first year of captivity, he'd fantasized returning home to Allie with his hands full of American Beauty roses. By the time eighteen months had passed, he'd come to the conclusion that roses were too commonplace for his wife. For what he felt for her. After several weeks intensive thought he'd switched to daisies, like the ones she'd always tried to grow in the apartment garden in Beirut. Sometime during the third year he decided daisies were too plain for his extraordinary bride.

During the following months the question of what type of flowers to arrive home with became more and more important. In truth, making the proper choice became an obsession, something to concentrate on during those times when he thought he might go mad. For a brief time he'd considered tulips, then concluded they'd only remind her of his abduction—not the mood he wanted to create.

Finally, last spring, he'd hit upon the perfect choice.

"Sorry," Haynes said, handing him the phone. "But if you still want the flowers, I'm sure the concierge can arrange for them to be waiting here in the suite for her."

"It's not the same thing," Mitch grumbled, nevertheless taking the telephone from the State Department official. Three minutes later he hung up, with the concierge's assurance that the flowers would arrive within the hour.

Business concluded, Mitch resumed his pacing. "I still don't understand why you guys are treating me like the spy who came in from the cold. I'm a reporter, not a CIA plant." It was the same thing he'd told his captives for five years. He hadn't been surprised when none of them believed him. From their point of view, any American still foolish enough to be hanging around that part of the world had to be an imperialist Yankee spy.

"Believe me, Cantrell," Haynes said, "if you *were* CIA, you'd still be tucked away in some safe house somewhere."

With an impatient mutter, Mitch stopped in front of the window, jamming his hands into the back pockets of his new dress slacks. They had been purchased for him in Germany, along with three shirts, underwear and another pair of shoes—soft Italian loafers that were almost as comfortable as his old faithful ones. The air force brass had not been about to send their charge back to America in the filthy jeans and torn T-shirt he'd been wearing when he'd walked in the door.

"So word of my release gets out. What's the big deal?"

Haynes's long sigh indicated he was getting extremely weary of arguing the subject. "Look, the White House isn't pleased with the information that's being leaked out of

Lebanon and Germany. It's my job to keep you under wraps until the diplomatic agenda has been settled."

Mitch threw his tall rangy frame onto the blue silk, French sofa. Frustration had him grinding his teeth. His headache was threatening to escalate into a full-fledged killer, and a giant fist was twisting his gut in two. "Diplomatic agenda, hell," he complained. "Why don't you guys just tell the truth? The president's looking toward the next election, and I'm the best photo op he's got this week."

Haynes didn't deny it. "All I know is that my orders are to see that you're comfortable and that you have everything you need until tomorrow morning's Rose Garden ceremony."

Mitch cursed quietly. "Has anyone considered that when I write about all this—and I will—I'm going to be obliged to point out that there isn't a great deal of difference between captivity in Lebanon and house arrest in our nation's capital?"

Haynes smiled at that. "Sure there is. For one thing, you can't get this stuff in Lebanon." He opened a small refrigerator, pulled out a chilled bottle of beer and tossed it to Mitch. "Why don't you just relax, Cantrell? Moaning at me isn't going to make your wife's plane get here any faster."

There'd been a time when Mitch wouldn't have put up with the government calling the shots like this. Stories of Mitch Cantrell's temper were legion, some exaggerated, most not, though Mitch didn't consider himself difficult. Driven, perhaps, but never difficult. He never had understood what was wrong with expecting people to do their best; after all, he certainly wasn't any harder on others than he was on himself.

He'd been born a newsman. When he was six, he had talked his aunt Helen into getting him a Junior Newsman's printing press. The type was rubber rather than metal, and each sheet of paper had to be individually stamped, but by the time he was eight years old, his weekly *Russian Hill Review* had a paid circulation of twenty-five subscribers. At ten he had three kids working for him as stringers and one hundred subscribers. Most of the *Review*'s readers took the paper for the gossip they gleaned from its six pages. Every Thursday morning people would sit down to their coffee and discover what their neighbors had been up to all week.

He was eleven years old when Kennedy was assassinated. After the grief-stricken principal of his school canceled classes for the remainder of the day, Mitch raced home with plans to put out a special edition of the *Review*. Complete with a black border, he'd decided, hoping that he had enough ink to pull it off. But when he'd arrived, his mother had been sitting in front of the television, her eyes red from weeping. Intending to comfort her for a few minutes before he got down to work, Mitch joined her on the sofa.

The special edition of the *Russian Hill Review* never got printed. Because for three long days its publisher, editor and star reporter sat riveted in front of the television screen watching events unfold live before his very eyes.

The next week he went to his bank, withdrew the money he'd been saving for a new platen printing press, bought a used eight-millimeter movie camera from a pawnshop down on Mission Street, and began roaming San Francisco in search of stories.

Once, while walking near Union Square, he happened by a jewelry shop just as it was being robbed by two armed gunmen. Never without his camera, with no thought for his own life, he filmed the robbers' getaway. When the local television station paid him for his film, his family and friends gathered in the Cantrell living room to watch Mitch's footage on the evening news. The moment he saw his film on the television screen, followed by his eyewitness interview with Reece Longworth, the station's anchorman, Mitch was hooked.

Over the years he'd been called a genius, a loner, a playboy and a bastard. Mitch had never cared what anyone called him, so long as they admitted he was "right." He had a worldwide network of impeccable sources that he could depend upon to give him whatever information he needed to break a big story. Which he did with unrelenting regularity. Critics and viewers alike routinely proclaimed him the most trustworthy newsman on television; the network brass, always looking for improved ratings, had offered him their top anchor spot more than once. Each time he'd turned it down.

Sitting behind a desk, reading copy written by someone else, was not his idea of a life. To spend his days locked in a New York office, never free to chase down a fast-breaking story, would be like being in prison, he'd claimed.

Well, he'd been in prison. And he hadn't liked it. Neither did he like playing by Alex Haynes's State Department rules.

Mitch took a long pull on the ice-cold beer. As it splashed against the back of his throat, he decided that it was almost as good as he'd been fantasizing. "What would you do if I just took off out that door?" he asked casually. "Shoot me in the back?"

Alex Haynes looked about as thrilled to be babysitting Mitch Cantrell as Mitch was to have him there. "That's a distinct possibility," he answered, careful to match Mitch's easy tone.

Mitch shrugged as he took another drink. "You'd never do it."

"Think not?" Haynes challenged quietly.

"Not on a bet," Mitch said. "You're a pacifist at heart, Haynes."

"Sounds as if you've got me all figured out."

"You're not that hard to figure," Mitch alleged. "You joined the foreign service, which shows a bent for adventure, but if you were the type of guy who thought that guns were the answer to the world's problems, you'd have signed on with military intelligence instead of the State Department." Finishing off the beer, he tossed the empty bottle into the leather wastepaper basket. "You're an endangered species in this town, Haynes—an idealist."

Before Haynes could decide whether or not he'd been insulted, Mitch added, "And if that isn't reason enough not to shoot me, a hero with a bullet in his back would probably be a bit difficult to explain to the press."

"Not the White House press," Haynes said. "They're so used to being fed stories, they've lost the investigative instinct."

Mitch laughed. How many times had he said exactly the same thing? He had no patience for quiescent lazy reporters, and considered beat-sweeteners—flattering news stories written solely to reward sources—on a par with checkbook journalism. Anyone who'd lower himself to write a puff piece should get out of the business and go to work in advertising, or even worse, public relations.

"Well, since it's obvious that you're going to stick to me like glue until tomorrow," he said with a sudden show of good-natured acceptance, "I have just one more question."

"What now?"

"Do you really think that bed in there is big enough for the three of us?"

"Three?"

"You, me, and my wife."

There was a long, uncomfortable silence as the color rose from beneath Haynes's collar. "I'd already planned to move into the room across the hall, once Mrs. Cantrell got here."

That was a surprise. Mitch had distinctly heard Haynes's superior instruct him to stay with their "guest" until after the Rose Garden ceremony.

Haynes gave Mitch a long level look. "I'm bending orders on this one, Mitch. If you decided to take off in the middle of the night, I may as well go back to Des Moines and go to work in my uncle's insurance agency, like my mom always wanted. Because the powers that be will make sure I'll never work in D.C. again."

Despite his irritation at having to wait for Allie's arrival, Mitch's smile was slow and decidedly wicked. "Don't worry, Haynes. Once I get my wife up here where she belongs, I'm not going to be in any hurry to go anywhere."

IT WAS RUSH HOUR. After fighting the snarl of commuter traffic, made worse by what Alanna considered to be a demonic traffic design, the limousine finally glided to a stop in front of the hotel. Exiting with Elizabeth, Alanna glanced around for the taxi Jonas had taken from the airport. They'd taken separate cars in the event that Mitch might be waiting in the lobby.

When she didn't see Jonas, she decided he must have become a victim of what the limousine driver had called "diplolock," a gridlock caused by a diplomatic motorcade down Constitution Avenue. One they'd been fortunate to just miss. She hoped Jonas wouldn't be stuck in traffic too long; although he'd proven incredibly supportive, she knew the situation had to be difficult for him.

Alanna had been surprised and disappointed when Mitch hadn't been at the airport to greet her, but Kyle Fields, who'd met their plane, explained that the White House was trying to avoid unnecessary publicity. Although she had no choice but to believe him, Alanna had spent the long frustrating ride to the hotel worrying that Mitch might have been too ill or too weak to come to the airport.

"I think you should see him first," Elizabeth said as they rode up in the elevator.

Alanna had prayed for this moment; she'd dreamed about it. But now that it was actually about to happen, she was suddenly scared to death. So much time had passed. So many things had changed since that day five years ago. She'd changed. And undoubtedly Mitch would have. What would they say to one another?

"Oh, no," she insisted quickly. "You're his mother, Elizabeth. You go first."

Elizabeth gave her a quick sharp look. "Alanna, you're not going to do anything foolish, are you?"

Alanna ran her hands through her hair, surprised to find them trembling. "Like walk in the suite and blurt out the fact that I'm getting married in less than three weeks, before any of us has time to say hello?"

"I know how difficult this is for you, dear," Elizabeth said, placing a well-manicured hand on her former daughter-in-law's arm. "But think how difficult life has been for Mitch these past years."

A shadow of annoyance stirred in Alanna's eyes. She cast a surreptitious glance toward the State Department official, who was looking up at the lighted numbers, seemingly oblivious to the personal conversation. But Alanna had the feeling that he wasn't missing a word. "I haven't been thinking of anything else since he called," she said quietly. "You don't have to worry, Elizabeth. I loved Mitch. I'd never do anything to hurt him."

"Loved? As in past tense?"

Alanna wondered why she should be feeling so defensive when it had been Elizabeth who'd been stressing the need for her to get on with her life. "I thought Mitch was dead."

"But he's not. Your husband is alive, Alanna."

Alanna was more than a little relieved when the elevator door suddenly opened, depriving her of an opportunity to answer. As their escort led them down the carpeted hallway to a set of double doors, Alanna's heart began to pound furiously.

The double doors opened, and she found herself face-to-face with the man she'd once adored more than anyone in the entire world. He looked different. But the same, Alanna decided. His blond hair was streaked with silver, but it added a certain flair, she thought. She'd expected him to be pale and wan, but his face, while thinner, was darkly tanned.

He'd lost weight. Mitch had never carried an ounce of excess fat, but now he seemed to be nothing but muscle and sinew. Lines fanned out from his eyes and there were deep gouges carved at either side of his mouth.

"I spent five years, thinking up the exact right thing to say when we were reunited," Mitch said, in that low, husky voice that had always thrilled her. "But now that you're actually here, I can't remember a single word."

He took her face into his hands and looked down at her. His heart was in his throat; it was all he could do not to start crying like a baby. "We have to stop meeting like this," he said in a vain attempt at flippancy.

Although she'd promised herself that she'd remain in control, traitorous tears filled Alanna's eyes. "Oh, Mitch." Without warning the dam burst and she began to sob.

Mitch wrapped his arms around her as she wept against his shoulder. He knew little about comforting women; his mother had always been a rock, and during their twelve, brief months of marriage, Alanna had proven consistently cheerful and agreeable. Since he couldn't think of any words that might ease the pain she was obviously feeling, he remained silent, stroking her back and murmuring soft inarticulate sounds of sympathy.

Elizabeth, watching the tender scene, relaxed for the first time since Alanna had arrived at her house with Jonas. And although she knew her own wet eyes revealed maternal longing, she crossed the room to the bar, gratefully accepting the drink Alex Haynes offered.

"Alex Haynes," he introduced himself. "State Department."

Elizabeth took a sip of scotch, relaxing ever so slightly as its warmth began to flow through her. "Elizabeth Cantrell," she said. "Mother."

In deference to the long-awaited reunion that was going on, they spoke quietly, but they could have been shouting at the top of their lungs for all Alanna and Mitch would have noticed. They were lost in a world of feelings, of emotions too complex to catalog as they stood together in the center of the room.

"I thought you were dead," she managed to say. "All these years."

Mitch held her tighter, drawing in her scent, which was as rich and complex as it was unfamiliar. "You should have known I wouldn't die," he said huskily. "Not when I had you to come home to."

What would he say, Alanna wondered miserably, when he discovered that she hadn't waited? Lifting her head, she looked up at him, her face twisted with anguish. "Oh, Mitch."

He brushed the tears off her cheeks with his fingertips; they were hot, as if they'd been burning behind her eyes for too long. "Shh," he soothed. "It's all over, Allie. We're together again. Forever."

When that threatened to release a new torrent of tears, Alanna garnered the strength to back away. Both physically and emotionally. Slipping out of his arms, she took a deep ragged breath. "You haven't said hello to your mother."

A question flickered in Mitch's eyes and his brow furrowed at the way Alanna had distanced herself from him, but deciding to unravel that little puzzle later, when he could dwell upon it, he turned toward Elizabeth.

"Hey, Mom. How about coming here and giving your prodigal son a hug?"

Elizabeth needed no second invitation. Putting down her drink on the bar, she threw her arms around his shoulders. "I always said that your stunts would make me old before my time," she scolded.

Her wobbly smile was the only sign of emotional turmoil. Feeling a surge of affection that washed away his earlier concern about Alanna, Mitch grinned down at his mother. For a fleeting moment his eyes danced with the devilish sparkle that had always possessed the power to charm women from eight to eighty. "Never. You're still the most gorgeous lady in San Francisco."

"And you're still incorrigible."

"Disappointed?"

"In you? Never." Going up onto her toes, she pressed a kiss against his cheek. "We've missed you, Mitchell."

Drawing her against him for a long comfortable moment, Mitch felt himself relaxing for the first time since
he'd been released three days ago. "Not as much as I missed
you," he said gruffly.

Releasing her, he rubbed his hands together and feigned
a jaunty eager attitude that belied the increasing pounding in his head. "I've ordered champagne," he said, opening the refrigerator beneath the bar. "And caviar. And
Scottish smoked-salmon for you, Allie." He flashed her a
smile. When she could only manage a weak smile in return, Mitch knew that his first instincts had been right.
Something was definitely wrong with her. She was too
quiet. Too pale.

"One glass," Elizabeth agreed. "And then I leave you
and Alanna alone."

Intent on opening the champagne, Mitch missed Alanna's look of panic.

ONE FLOOR ABOVE Mitch and Alanna's suite, Jonas was
pacing the floor like a caged lion. Had it only been last
night that he'd been at Elizabeth's party, anticipating
making love to his fiancée? He'd been thinking of his marriage and the sun-gilded halcyon years he and Alanna were
going to share. Then that damn phone call had come and
all his plans—hell, his entire life—had gone spiraling out
of control. He felt as if he were on a runaway freight train.

If there was one thing Jonas hated, it was not being in
total control. Not that he was one of those people who
planned his entire life, moment by moment, day by day,
year by year. Experience had taught him how to punt.

The oldest of six children and the only son, he'd been
twelve years old when his father, a San Francisco police-
man with six months left until retirement, had been
gunned down in a shoot-out between two rival China-

town gangs. Since raising six kids on a patrolman's salary hadn't allowed any extra money for savings, Mary Harte, a high school music teacher, began teaching piano lessons in the evenings and on Saturdays. Jonas immediately stepped into the role of surrogate father to his five younger sisters. He also took over all the household chores, which not only made him a good cook, but the only sixteen-year-old boy on the block who could successfully iron the smocking on a size 6X, dotted swiss, Sunday school dress.

Since the Harte's rambling home was in continual need of repair, Jonas had also learned to be handy. For a time he'd considered working in construction, but Mary had insisted that his father had always dreamed of him going to college. It was then that he decided he could perhaps find a future in architecture.

An athletic scholarship, along with a grant from the Policemen's Benevolent Association, paved his way to the University of California, Berkeley, where he played on the football team as a defensive lineman. His numbers were so impressive that by his junior year he had garnered considerable interest from pro scouts, until a knee injury in the final game of the season effectively ended his dreams of a professional football career.

Quickly adapting to this new change in his career plans, Jonas, an academic All-American, won a summer architectural internship with a prestigious San Francisco firm and after graduation immediately went to work, helping to design towering buildings that would become a vital part of the San Francisco skyline.

About the same time his mother remarried. Benjamin Douglas was a wealthy securities attorney in Pacific Heights. Professing a lifelong dream to play jazz piano, he'd signed up for private lessons three nights a week. And although his decided lack of talent would forever keep him off the concert stage, within weeks Benjamin and Mary Harte were—together—beginning to make music of another kind. Jonas had not resented his mother remarrying. On the contrary, he'd gladly handed the fatherly duties over to Benjamin, who relished the role.

Five years after joining the architectural firm, Jonas was awarded a coveted partnership. For eight long and profitable years he managed to convince himself that he was happy in the corporate world. After all, his name was well-known in architectural circles, his fees were equal to those of his highly successful attorney stepfather, and he'd even been profiled in *The Wall Street Journal* as one of the new, exciting breed of city builders.

But something within him struggled against the constraints of the corporate world, and although he was fortunate enough to live, in his opinion, in the most beautiful city in the world, his workaholic attitude precluded any free time to enjoy all that San Francisco had to offer.

Perhaps it was because he'd done nothing but work for too many years. Or perhaps it was due to his sister Janice finding a lump in her breast, the day before her twenty-eighth birthday. The tumor turned out to be benign, but the sudden realization that sometimes life didn't wait for you to catch up made Jonas decide that he was due for a change.

Resigning his partnership in the firm, he sublet his sleek penthouse apartment, moved onto a boat in Sausalito and started a new business renovating San Francisco's Victorian homes. His business flourished, while still allowing him time to go sailing, fishing and backpacking. He only took work that interested him, jobs that presented a unique challenge. His hours were his own and he doubted that he wore a suit more than three times a year.

And best of all, Jonas thought, his work was directly responsible for his meeting Alanna. If he'd been the kind of man who believed in tea leaves and fortune-tellers, he might have suspected that their falling in love had been preordained.

Jonas stared out the window at the steady drizzle. Under normal circumstances he enjoyed the rain. Enjoyed the sound of it on the roof of his boat, its fresh scent, the feeling of renewal it left behind. But there was nothing normal about tonight. Because the woman he loved—the woman he intended to marry—was downstairs, sharing an intimate reunion with her husband.

5

SOMETHING was definitely out of kilter. Mitch had been a reporter too long not to know when someone was trying to hide something. And whatever was eating away at Allie had to be really big.

"Alone at last," he said, after Elizabeth and Haynes had retired to their own rooms.

Tell him, a little voice in the back of her mind coaxed. *Before the air gets any thicker*. Alanna rubbed her hands on her suit skirt. "If you don't mind," she said in a small, strained voice, "I'd like to freshen up. It's been a hectic day, and I must look a mess."

Mitch caught her nervous hand. "You look lovely." When his fingers circled her wrist, he felt her pulse jump. "Black suits you," he said, running the fingers of his free hand over the lapel of her jacket.

The chic suit was a long way from the airy pastel dresses he remembered her favoring. In a strange way, it made him feel as if she was a stranger. But that was ridiculous, Mitch told himself. He'd known Allie since she was a little girl. Hell, he could even remember comforting her the day she got her braces, assuring her that any boy with any imagination could manage to figure out a way to kiss her past all that hardware.

"I never imagined you in black," he said truthfully. "But you were right to choose it, because the color sets off your skin in a way that makes a man want to touch it." His knuckles trailed up her cheek. "Taste it." He bent his head, his intent obvious. Alanna took a step back. "Allie?"

Unable to face the confusion in his gaze, she pointedly avoided his eyes. "I really need to freshen up," she said again in a strangled voice.

If Mitch hadn't known better, he would have thought she was scared to death. But that was nonsense. So what was the problem?

The events of the past three days were beginning to catch up with him and Mitch found himself suddenly too weary to try to unravel the puzzle now. The pounding in his head was beginning to reach epic proportions, and the churning in his gut made him wish he'd foregone that beer.

"Just don't take too long." His husky, seductive tone took a major effort. While his mind was more than willing, his traitorous body was proving distractingly weak. "Because we've got a lot of catching up to do, sweetheart."

Feeling like a crab scuttling away in the sand, Alanna escaped to the bathroom. Leaning back against the locked door, she squeezed her eyes shut, as if to steel herself against the questions she'd seen swirling in the depths of his tired, but still vivid blue eyes. "Oh, God," she whispered raggedly, "what am I going to do?"

Taking a deep breath, she splashed some water onto her face, touched up her makeup, ran a brush through her hair, then confronted her reflection in the mirror.

"Smile," she commanded her ashen image. "This is supposed to be a happy day."

And it was. Under normal conditions, the fact that Mitch had returned, alive and relatively unharmed from all those years of captivity, would have been a dream come true. A miracle. Unfortunately, the timing couldn't have been worse. Because nine months ago, Jonas Harte had come into her life, opening doors she'd thought she'd locked forever, enabling her to fall in love again—with him.

Dragging her hands through her hair, she straightened her shoulders, took another deep breath and left the bathroom.

Mitch was standing by the window, looking down onto Connecticut Avenue. His back was turned toward her, allowing her the opportunity to observe him undetected. He definitely was thinner, Alanna determined. But he was not as emaciated as she would have expected, given what he must have suffered. His silvered hair was shaggy, but showed the signs of having been cut—albeit poorly—in the past few months. All in all, from outward appearances, he might have returned from nothing more debilitating than a particularly rigorous time roughing it in the wilderness. But there was something else, something far more telling.

It was the way he was standing, shoulders hunched, head bowed, that made her heart contract. He looked, she decided, strangely lost. Alanna had never seen her husband anything other than eminently confident, in total control, not only of himself, but the world around him, as well. She'd always marveled that Mitch was one of those rare individuals who could be thrown into absolute chaos, anywhere in the world, and manage to radiate an aura of supreme self-reliance. It was, she mused, one of the things that had fueled his meteoric rise to the pinnacle of an intensely competitive profession.

She was trying to think of something—anything—to say, when an enormous basket of flowers on a nearby table caught her eye. "Oh, Mitch."

He turned and forced a jaunty smile. "I sure hope you still like wildflowers." When he'd placed the call to the concierge earlier this afternoon, he'd been entirely satisfied with his decision. More than satisfied—smug. But that was before he'd witnessed this new, strangely sophisticated Allie. The Allie of the sleek haircut, the stark black suit, the complex, but undeniably stirring scent.

The flowers were a riot of colors and sweet perfumes. As she met his loving gaze over the bright blossoms, Alanna knew Mitch was sharing the romantic memories the flowers evoked.

SHE HAD JUST RECEIVED her master's degree when Mitch returned home from Lebanon for his father's funeral. Although the occasion was admittedly a sad one, there was nothing unhappy about the way Mitch made Alanna feel. Every time he looked at her. Smiled at her. Touched her.

Mitch himself had been no less affected. Putting in for some back vacation time—caught up in the events unfolding day by day in the Middle East, he hadn't taken any time off for the past two years—he began to pursue Alanna with the same damn-the-torpedoes, full-steam-ahead enthusiasm he'd always applied to his work.

He'd been home for five days when they went on a drive down the Monterey Coast. The scenery along the rugged coastline was magnificent, but Alanna had not paid any heed to the rugged cliffs and the wild, white-capped surf sculpting the coastline. Instead all her attention had been riveted on Mitch, on the smallest of details—the way his long fingers curved around the leather steering wheel, the way the muscles of his long legs flexed and relaxed beneath his denim jeans as he worked the clutch, the way the sharp aroma of pine soap filled her head.

After a time, he pulled off the highway onto a gravel road that twisted and turned through the Santa Lucia mountains. Eventually the gravel gave way to dirt, but still

Mitch kept driving. Alanna didn't care where they were going. It was enough to be alone with him. She knew that this holiday would not go on indefinitely; soon he'd be returning to his work on the other side of the world. For now she wanted to savor every delicious moment.

"Oh dear," she murmured, when the road came to an end at a wooden gate. On the gate was posted a No Trespassing sign.

"No problem." Mitch climbed out of the car and opened the gate.

"Are you sure we should do this?" she asked, after he'd driven through the gateway, stopping again briefly to close the barrier behind them. Her expression was grave, her eyes filled with worry. Alanna was obviously one of those people who'd consider jaywalking a capital crime, Mitch decided. Accustomed to short-lived affairs with newswomen who were more than willing to camp all over a quarry's front yard, if that was what it took to get a story, Mitch found Alanna's concern for propriety delightful.

"I did a story on the Navajo-Hopi land dispute in Arizona a few years ago." He continued driving up the twisting dirt road.

"I know. I saw it," Alanna said. In truth, she had never missed one of his special reports.

Mitch decided that he rather liked the idea of Allie watching him. "Then you might remember that Hopi elder who said that no man can actually own the land. We merely borrow it from our gods. And from future generations."

She did remember. Indeed, at the time, and under the circumstances involved, Alanna had found such a tenet an admirable belief. But unfortunately, criminal trespassing laws were based on an entirely different doctrine. "Still—"

"Allie. Don't worry." He ran a hand down her hair, long silky chestnut hair that fell straight as rainwater down her back. "We won't be arrested and thrown in the slammer. I know the owner of the property."

It would have been impossible to miss the humor in his tone. "Are you laughing at me?"

"Never," he insisted immediately. Pulling the car over to the side of the road, he turned toward her and ran a slow, seductive hand down her face. "Because what you've done to me, sweetheart, is no laughing matter."

She watched, her heart in her throat as he slowly lowered his head, his intent obvious. His lips whispered against her softly parted ones, like the brush of exquisite silk against bare flesh, barely touching as his fingers stroked her neck and hair. "Allie." His breath was warm against her skin; his lips skimmed up her cheeks, lingering tantalizingly at her temples, her eyelids, her earlobe. "Do you have any idea how much I want you?"

When his mouth returned to hers, the breath she had been unaware of holding shuddered out. "Oh, yes." His teeth nipped at her lower lip; common sense disintegrated. "Because I want you, too." She twined her fingers through his thick, sandy hair. "I love you, Mitch."

Love. For a man who had always considered himself fearless, he'd run for years from that word, thinking it a burden that would slow him down, interfere with his work. His life. But now Mitch decided that he'd never heard any words so sweet.

She leaned toward him, her breasts pressing against the front of his shirt, generating an ache deep in his loins. Although Mitch was nearly overcome by a sudden impulse to drag her onto his lap and take her here, now, he forced himself to remember that he'd brought her here to create a memory. A rich, sensual memory that they would carry with them for the rest of their lives. He wasn't about to make love to her for the first time on the seat of the car, like some oversexed teenager.

"Allie. Sweetheart." He captured both her hands in his and lifted them to his lips. "This is impossible."

Color flooded her cheeks. What in the world had gotten into her, blurting out her innermost feelings? Mitch Cantrell was accustomed to women with whom he could share a night of passion without getting himself tied up in a tangle of romantic strings. So what had she done? Professed her love like a foolish schoolgirl.

"I'm sorry," she managed through lips that had turned to stone. "It just slipped out." She forced a shaky laugh. "I don't know why. It's not as if I meant it. . . . I mean, gracious, Mitch, I'm not the kind of woman who mistakes sexual desire for . . . well, you know . . ." Her voice faded as she realized she couldn't—wouldn't—say that dangerous word again.

"For love?" Mitch asked quietly.

A blue jay was scolding them from a nearby tree branch. Unnerved by Mitch's intent, unwavering gaze, Alanna turned away and tried desperately to focus on the bright blue bird.

But Mitch was not about to let her get away so easily. Cupping her chin in his fingers, he turned her head back toward him. "Is that all you're feeling, Allie?" When he touched her face, not seductively, as he had earlier, but possessively, Alanna shivered. "Sex? Desire? Lust?"

Because she couldn't lie, Alanna said, "I'm afraid."

Looking thoughtful, he twined a lock of her hair around his hand. She was wearing a full-skirted, white eyelet sundress. Although its front cut demurely across her shoulder blades, the back plunged to the waist, revealing a breathtaking expanse of creamy skin. The effect was both virginal and sexy. Like her. Mitch found the contrast irresistible.

"So am I."

That was a surprise. It was difficult to imagine Mitch Cantrell—the man who'd gone into Afghanistan disguised as a rebel fighter, the man who'd made worldwide headlines when he'd been the only reporter on the scene of a Latin American coup—the same man who'd single-handedly managed to infiltrate a secret PLO stronghold in Beirut—to be afraid of anyone or anything. The fact that he might be afraid of her was too incredible for words.

"I don't think I believe that," she said finally.

His answering smile was warm, but tinged with a seriousness she found unnerving. "It's true. Because you're important, Allie. What I feel for you is important."

Struck mute by the implication behind his words, Alanna could only stare at him.

"Will you trust me?" he asked suddenly. Intensity deepened his voice, glowed brightly in his eyes.

Alanna licked her suddenly dry lips. "Always."

"Good." Before Alanna could perceive his intent, Mitch had released her, exited the car, come around to the passenger side and opened her door. "It's a beautiful day. Let's take a walk."

Although it was not her first choice, Alanna smiled. "I'd love to."

They walked hand in hand down a winding, tree-lined path, through a shaded grove to the edge of a precipice. Far below, the full fury of the Pacific Ocean pounded against the worn granite cliffs.

"It's so incredibly beautiful," she murmured. "In a wild, untamed way." And it fitted her mood perfectly. The thundering refrain of the surf seemed to echo the out-of-control hammering of her heart.

"There's no place like it in the world," Mitch agreed.

"And I suppose you should know." Alanna couldn't help thinking of all the exotic places he'd been. Places he would go again. She could no longer keep quiet; she had to ask the question that had been plaguing her for days. "When do you have to go back to Beirut?"

Even as Alanna was priding herself on the way she'd kept her tone calm, Mitch had seen the flash of pain in her soft green eyes. It would be so easy to lie, he considered, turning his gaze out to sea, where a lone gull cruised low over the churning surf.

"Soon." The sea gull dived, disappearing for a moment, before returning with a flash of silver in its beak. "Actually," he admitted, "the network called last night."

Her heart lurched, but she forced herself to remain matter-of-fact. "Oh?" The wind danced at the eyelet hem of her skirt, the sea crashed below.

"There are rumors of a cease-fire, maybe even a peace accord, circulating over there. Although I'm convinced that they're nothing more than another false alarm, it wouldn't do for the network's hotshot reporter to be cooling his heels in the States when and if peace finally came."

"I can understand that." Alanna could. But that didn't mean she had to like it. She sighed before she could prevent it. "When do you leave?"

Well, Mitch considered, it was now or never. "Tomorrow."

"So soon." It was not a question.

"I'm afraid so." He turned toward her, putting both hands upon her shoulders. His eyes, as they searched hers, seemed to be filled with questions. Just when Alanna thought that he was going to say something, he shook his head with ill-concealed frustration. His palms slid down her arms, his fingers linked with hers. "I want to make love with you, Allie."

Dear Lord, she wanted that, too. Even now that she knew there would be no future between them. Because if Mitch was going to get onto that plane and fly out of her life tomorrow, she wanted memories of this special time they'd shared.

"Yes." Lifting their linked hands, she pressed them between her breasts. "Here. Now."

Her flesh, even beneath the cotton bodice of her sundress, felt warm and inviting. Mitch needed every bit of self-restraint he possessed to shake his head. "It's too dangerous."

"I'm in a mood to live dangerously."

Despite the slow ache in his loins, Mitch laughed. "So am I. But even I'm not foolhardy enough to try to make love to my girl on the edge of a cliff." He wanted to kiss her, but his control was hanging by a thread, and he knew that all it would take was one taste of her sweet, succulent lips to snap it. "Come on," he insisted in a voice that was a long way from his usual controlled one. "We're almost there."

Her blood pounding in her ears, Alanna continued walking with him along the rugged cliffs. A monarch butterfly flew in front of them, its orange-and-black wings fluttering as it fought the stiff sea breeze. After a while, the path turned away from the precipice, disappearing into another grove of trees. Then they turned a corner and Alanna found herself facing a sea of color. Although they were no longer on the cliff, she could hear the soft roar of the surf echoing in the distance.

"I've never seen so many wildflowers in one place."

"Isn't it remarkable?"

"It's the most beautiful place I've ever seen." Alanna felt awe widen her eyes as she stared at the profusion of riotous hues. In the trees overhead the birds flittered from limb to limb, as if playing a game of musical branches. "How did you ever find it?"

"A friend of mine told me about it."

"The friend who owns this property?"

"The very same. The way he described it, I knew it would be special." The breeze was softer, gentler here. It feathered Alanna's hair, blowing wispy tendrils against her cheeks. Her gaze held by Mitch, she saw him reach out and brush away a few errant chestnut strands. The soft touch of his fingers made her blood hum. "Like you."

For a fleeting moment, Alanna wondered how many women he'd called special. How many women he'd made love to in a bed of wildflowers. But then he drew her closer, causing her blood's rhythm to pick up speed and her body to soften against his.

"Allie." His lips skimmed over her face, heatedly, hungrily, drinking in the exquisite taste of her skin. "My Allie."

The sheer possessiveness in his husky tone was her undoing. Her heart opened, and she kissed him with all the love that welled up inside her. She wanted to give him anything, everything he wanted.

This time he wasn't gentle. He wanted to be. Mitch was a man who did everything skillfully. Including making love. All the way up here he'd promised himself that he'd go slow, first seducing her with the exquisite scenery, then with soft words, then with tender hands that would pleasure her in ways she'd never imagined. But he hadn't counted on her generosity. On the way she opened herself, gave herself to him so freely. He hadn't expected his thoughts to cloud like this or his body to ache with such intensity.

He wanted to crush, to devour, to claim. As their tongues tangled, it was too easy to forget that in just a few, short hours he was going to be on a plane, bound for Beirut. As her breath flowed warmly out of her, he forgot that he'd never wanted a permanent woman in his life. He felt his name murmured against his mouth and wondered why he'd always thought love a hindrance. A trap to be avoided, at all cost. But all that had changed. Because of Allie.

While the soft breeze sighed through the branches of the trees overhead, Mitch lowered the zipper of her sundress, causing it to whisper over her body as it drifted to the ground. When she heard him catch his breath, she felt a dangerous, almost wanton pride. He wanted her; she could see it in his eyes, could feel it in the slight trembling of his fingers, as they dispensed with the ribbon closure of the lacy fantasy she'd worn under the dress.

"You are so beautiful, you leave me speechless." Alanna's heart skipped a beat when his hand covered it. "And for me, that's definitely a first." The hand at her breast caressed, fondled, tormented.

Without taking her eyes from his, Alanna slowly unbuttoned his shirt. She pushed it off his shoulders, and it fluttered to the ground to lie atop her dress. He was the one who was beautiful, Alanna decided as she tentatively ran her palms down his dark chest, over his rigid, washboardlike stomach. He was strong and hard and so undeniably male. So perfect. What could she offer a man like this?

Suddenly terrified that she'd end up disappointing him, she wrapped her arms around his waist and pressed her cheek against his chest. Mitch felt the change in her immediately. "Allie?" he murmured against the top of her head. "What's wrong, sweetheart?"

If she didn't go through with this, he was going to think her the world's biggest tease. If she did, and couldn't live up to his expectations—up to the expertise of his other women—she didn't know how she'd ever face him again. Feeling foolish as well as frightened, she could only shake her head.

He stroked her back soothingly, feeling the fine muscles contract beneath his touch. She was tense. Too tense. "I'd never pressure you into doing anything you didn't want to, Allie."

It was getting worse by the minute. "No," she said, in a voice barely above a whisper. "I want to, Mitch, really, but . . ."

"If it's protection you're worried about, sweetheart—"

"No." What was wrong with her? She wasn't inexperienced. She'd been on the pill since her freshman year of college. So why was she suddenly behaving like a panicky virgin? "You don't have to worry about that."

The sudden, unexpected jolt of jealousy caused by her quiet admission startled Mitch. He'd never been one of those men who viewed an untouched woman as a challenge, a prize to capture. He had always preferred women of experience, willing to share an easy sexual relationship. No strings attached.

"Then what's the problem?" He skimmed his hands up and down her sides; his fingers teased her waist, her ribs, her breasts.

Exhaling a deep, shuddering breath, she tilted back her head to meet his curious gaze. "I'm afraid I won't be able to please you."

Alanna saw a myriad of emotions wash over Mitch's handsome features: shock, disbelief, then something so warm and tender it took her breath away. "Why don't you let me worry about that?" Taking her face into his hands, he lowered his mouth to hers. A soft sigh of pleasure slipped from between her lips to his as they slowly lowered themselves to the ground.

Exhibiting a patience he'd never known he possessed, Mitch loved her for a long, delicious time with only his mouth. As his lips tempted, cajoled, caressed, Alanna found herself trusting him as she'd trusted no other man. Closing her eyes, she allowed her mind to empty.

Caught up in the wonder of her, Mitch forced himself to go slowly, to savor every sigh, every soft moan. Buttery sunlight filtered through the leaves of the trees overhead, dappling her flawless skin with golden highlights. Rocking back onto his heels, Mitch gazed at the picture she made, lying in the bed of wildflowers, her hair fanned out around her, her eyes closed, a small womanly smile teasing the corners of her voluptuous lips. She looked delightfully wanton. Delicious. He'd never wanted a woman more. He'd never needed a woman more.

Feeling his heated gaze, Alanna slowly opened her eyes, thrilled by the hunger on his face. When she held out her arms, it was all the invitation he needed. Their remaining clothes were whisked away, as if by the sea breeze. Flesh warmed flesh. Soft sighs became moans. The inner fire built.

Alanna whispered words of pleasure into his ear, while Mitch planted kisses, passionate kisses, all over her fluid body. He delighted in the way her skin bloomed under his lips, the way she trembled under his touch, the way she welcomed everything he did to her.

Alanna's laugh, rich and smoky, floated on the perfumed air. Her hair wrapped around him, like sable silk against his flesh. It was torment. It was heaven. Agony.

Ecstasy. Yesterday vanished, tomorrow dimmed. There
was only now. Only this mad, greedy present.

When she arched against him, Mitch knew there could
be no more waiting. Gasping her name, he thrust into her.
Beneath him, her body was hot and moist and moving.
Their lovemaking echoed the force of the surf pounding
against the rocks as they rode the cresting waves of passion, giving completely to each other, holding nothing
back as they took one another far beyond reason.

ALANNA CLOSED HER EYES against the flood of memories.
Despite the fact that she'd had two previous lovers before
that day in the meadow, despite the fact that she'd been
twenty-four years old, she'd been incredibly naive. So innocent. And she'd adored Mitch more than life itself.

"I suppose every woman should be swept off her feet at
least once in her life," she murmured, more to herself than
to Mitch.

Mitch had watched the emotions on her face and knew
that she was no less affected by the memories the wildflowers had triggered than he. That, at least, he decided,
was something.

"I think we were both swept off our feet that day." He
closed the gap between them. His arms wrapped loosely,
unthreateningly, around her waist. "To be honest, I took
you up there to seduce you. But after we made love, I decided it was you who had seduced me."

"Perhaps we were both seduced," she said gently. "By
the scenery, the mood, and the fact that you were leaving
the next day."

There was something else in her voice. Something he
hadn't counted on. Regret? "My leaving may have contributed to me convincing you to elope that night," he admitted. "But believe me, Allie, if I hadn't fallen head over

heels in love with you, I could have walked away without a backward glance." He'd certainly done it before. Numerous times. But as he'd lain amid the flowers, basking in the cooling aftermath of passion, Mitch had realized that walking away from Allie would be no easy task. A man of quick decisions, he'd concluded that marriage was the only solution.

"I'm glad you didn't," she said truthfully. Because despite all that had happened, Alanna knew she'd always cherish that blissful, albeit rocky year she'd spent as Mitchell Cantrell's bride.

It was exactly what he'd been waiting to hear. "Me, too."

He pulled her close. Too close. For a moment her body—and her mind—responded to the once familiar touch. But when Mitch's lips skimmed up the side of her face, Alanna thought of Jonas.

"Mitch." Her mind reeled, struggling to come up with a delicate refusal. The questions were back in his eyes, along with a masculine frustration that he didn't bother to conceal. Attempting to placate him, Alanna lifted a trembling hand to his cheek.

His skin was hot. More than hot. It was flaming, and not with desire. "You're ill!"

Mitch breathed in the unfamiliar scent of Alanna's perfume, a dark, seductive scent that seemed to emanate from her pores. It was a toss-up which was throbbing more, his head or his groin.

"It's just a bug," he said with forced nonchalance. "I think I picked it up in Wiesbaden."

"Have you seen a doctor?"

"Yeah." His palms shaped her shoulders, and he wondered when she'd taken to wearing pads in her jackets. Although she was more beautiful than ever, she was beginning to remind him of Joan Crawford in all those early

career-woman movies on the late show. He'd always preferred Hedy Lamarr and her sarong.

"So? What did the doctor say?"

She moved only slightly, but he felt the distance widen.
"Nothing."

"Nothing?"

Mitch didn't want to talk. It seemed as if he'd been talking for days, ever since his release. Now all he wanted to
do was make love to his wife. "I didn't have it when I had
my physical at the base hospital."

Alanna pressed the back of her hand against Mitch's
forehead. "You really are burning up. I'm calling Alex
Haynes. He'll know a doctor."

Unwilling to throw in the towel completely, Mitch ran
his hands seductively down her arms. "I'll be fine. Really."

"Of course you will," she reassured, pulling away to go
to the telephone. "As soon as you receive proper medical
care."

She reminded him uncomfortably of a silken bulldozer. When had she become such a frustratingly stubborn woman? Mitch wondered, remembering a time when
Allie had willingly deferred to him on every decision, no
matter how trivial. Knowing when he was licked, Mitch
slumped dejectedly onto the sofa and watched her place
the call.

"Welcome home," he muttered.

6

IT WAS ALMOST MIDNIGHT when Alanna managed to get away.

"It's about time," Jonas said, opening the door an instant after she knocked. "Do you have any idea how crazy I've been, wondering what the hell was going on down there?" He decided not to elaborate on a few of the more disagreeable scenarios he'd imagined.

He was angry. She could see the temper in his eyes, a temper he managed to rein in. Her own control hanging by a whisper, Alanna sank onto the sofa. Because her breathing was still jerky, it took her a moment to answer.

"It wasn't exactly a picnic for me, either, Jonas," she reminded him quietly.

He wanted to shake her for the hell she'd put him through, these past agonizing hours. He wanted to hold her, comfort her for the distress he knew she must be feeling. Most of all he wanted to take her to bed. And what? Jonas asked himself. Stake his claim to her?

Yes, dammit. As ridiculous as it sounded, that was precisely what he wanted to do. Jonas had the grace to wince as he realized what Alanna would undoubtedly think of such a primitive male rationalization.

Garnering control of his own runaway emotions, Jonas took a long, judicial look at Alanna, searching for clues as to how the reunion had gone. That she was exhausted was obvious. Fatigue and pain darkened her eyes, and

tension he hadn't seen since the early days of their relationship was cutting deep lines into her forehead.

"I'm sorry. That was incredibly insensitive." He picked
up the bottle of brandy he'd ordered from room service
earlier. "Would you like a drink?"

"Just a small one, thanks."

She watched him pour the liquor, noting that he'd
barely touched the brandy himself, despite his obvious
anxiety. That was so like him, she thought. Unlike Mitch,
who often gave in to impulse, Jonas was a man of metic-
ulous thought and judicial reason; he was not likely to lose
control, however tiresome the situation. Another man
might have spent these past hours getting quietly—or not
so quietly—drunk. But not Jonas.

"Here you go." Their fingers brushed when he handed
her the glass and, emotionally wrung out though she was,
Alanna could not ignore the rush of excitement the casual
gesture created. He sat down upon the arm of the sofa.
"So, how is he?"

Alanna took a sip of brandy. "He's in the hospital."

"What? When did this happen?"

"A few hours ago. He's come down with some sort of
bug. The doctor said it's probably nothing serious, that
after five years he's simply lost his immunity to common
western viruses. But he still wanted to admit him for ob-
servation."

"I suppose that makes sense." Jonas was stroking her
hair, because he couldn't bear to have her this close and
not touch her. "How bad is it?"

"He's got a fever, but the doctor assured me that it wasn't
serious. I suggested putting off tomorrow's Rose Garden
Ceremony until he was feeling better, but of course Mitch
wouldn't listen."

Had he ever? Alanna wondered. Mitch had been exciting, romantic, dashing, and he'd made her feel like the most beautiful, desirable woman in the world. But had he ever shown serious concern for her wishes?

"Well, at least he hasn't lost the old fire."

Alanna sighed. "Emotionally and psychologically he seems like the same old Mitch. Although logic tells me that's impossible."

"An ordeal like he's been through would be bound to leave scars."

"That's what I've been telling myself." She let out a little breath, trying to relax. "Do you know, I came here today expecting him to be..."

Words seemed to fail her, and she dragged her hand through her hair. When Jonas noticed that she'd exchanged the diamond solitaire he'd bought her for a wide gold wedding band, ice skimmed down his spine, but he forced himself to wait until she'd finished her story.

"I don't know," she continued quietly. "I suppose I thought I'd find an empty shell of a man. Or at least an angry one, and I'd be furious, not only at the terrorists, but probably our government as well." Fire rose in her eyes, brief, but hot.

Jonas knew that Alanna had always considered the government's policy of refusing to deal with hostage takers as nothing less than abandoning the hostages. She'd made a second career—an unpaid one—of speaking out for hostage rights.

"Sounds like a fairly normal reaction."

"You'd think so, wouldn't you? But if Mitch is angry, he's certainly learned how to hold his temper."

Jonas had heard tales of Mitch Cantrell's infamous temper. Not from Alanna. There had been times when his heated battles with the network had nearly overshadowed the stories he'd been sent to cover. "That's not really very surprising," Jonas said. "He's a sharp guy, Alanna. It obviously didn't take him long to figure out that it paid to keep his mouth shut."

Images of torture flashed through her mind. Alanna shivered. "I've always thought of myself as an honest person."

"You are."

"I was." She put a hand over her eyes. "You know, despite Elizabeth's misgivings, I came here today prepared to tell Mitch everything right away. I thought that in the long run, it would be better to get things out in the open."

Jonas realized that he'd never understood fear until this moment. He wanted to touch her. Hold her. Pull her into his arms, take her to bed and never let her go. Knowing the futility of stopping this runaway train they were all on, he forced himself to be content with merely playing with the ends of her hair. "But?"

"But now that I've seen Mitch, talked with him, I'm beginning to realize that nothing about this is going to be simple or straightforward."

He could hear the emotion trembling in her voice. Although it took a major effort, Jonas put his own needs, his own desires aside. For now.

"It won't be easy," he agreed. "But you're a tough lady, sweetheart. You'll get through it." When she would have looked away, he caught her chin in his hand. "We'll get through it together."

Jonas was a rock, Alanna considered. And a rock was exactly what she needed right now. Just when she was thinking how lucky she was to have him, he gave her a long, searching look that made her feel he'd seen all the way to her soul.

"I know how upset you are, Alanna," he said. "And if there's one thing I don't want to do is dump any more pressure on you, but there's something I have to ask."

His expression was serious, which certainly wasn't surprising, given the circumstances. What did surprise Alanna was the unexpected vulnerability she viewed in his eyes.

"After all I've put you through the past forty-eight hours, I'd say you're entitled to ask anything you want, Jonas."

"Do you still love him?"

It should have been a simple question. But it wasn't. Alanna squeezed her eyes shut for a moment. "Oh, Jonas."

He'd marveled at Alanna's strength. For nine months he'd watched as she'd thrown herself into her editorial job, imprinting a style all her own upon the magazine. And she'd continued in her efforts to get the hostages in the Middle East freed. He couldn't count the number of times during their courtship she'd stood him up for dinner in order to fly to Washington, London, Paris, Rome, even Jerusalem.

The Alanna Cantrell he'd met and fallen in love with was a sleek, sophisticated, beautiful dynamo. In contrast, the woman who was sitting beside him now suddenly seemed small. Defenseless. He slipped his arm around her and pulled her close. Breathing a deep sigh, Alanna let her head rest on his shoulder and tried again to relax.

"I really had planned to tell him, Jonas, but he's so tired. And sick. And then, whenever I thought about ruining that Rose Garden ceremony tomorrow, I just couldn't do it."

"So that's why you took off your engagement ring."

Alanna looked guiltily at her left hand. "I couldn't welcome him home, flashing a diamond."

"Granted. But do you have any idea how I feel, seeing the woman I love wearing some other man's ring?"

"I didn't know what shape Mitch might be in," she protested. "I thought it would be best to break it to him gently. If he noticed that I wasn't wearing my wedding ring, he'd be bound to ask questions. And I wasn't sure he'd be strong enough to hear the answers."

Jonas understood. Really he did. But dammit, that didn't mean he had to like it. He drew her even closer, as if to shield her from more pain. "We don't have to talk about that now. Just try to unwind." He pressed his lips against her hair. "Things will look better in the morning."

"Do you think they could look any worse?"

Jonas managed a smile. The first of the day. "Of course," he said matter-of-factly. "You could have done the sensible thing nine months ago and bought yourself a modern, dependable house. Then we never would have met." He lifted her hand and kissed her fingers.

The lightning-flash thrill of desire that such a gentle kiss instilled shook Alanna to the core. She'd never experienced such edgy passion around Jonas before. Until last night. When all the hunger she'd suppressed, all the desires she had safely locked away for so many years had exploded, in one explosive torrent of heat. Feeling her reaction, Jonas lowered his head.

"I've been waiting for this all day." His deep voice vibrated against the sensitized skin of her lips.

He tasted without pressure, taking his time to kiss her parted lips from one tingling corner to the other. Alanna told herself that she should back away from this exquisite temptation. That she should leave now, before things got out of hand. But she couldn't move.

"We can't do this."

"But we are." His thumb trailed under her chin, holding her lightly. "And very well, too, if I do say so myself."

His mouth was warm, but soothing. And very, very sweet. Without breaking the exquisite contact of their lips, he slid off the arm of the sofa onto the cushion beside her. He unbuttoned the jacket of her suit and slipped it off her shoulders, revealing a silk teddy. The lacy black froth accented the stark lines of the suit; drinking in the sight, Jonas realized her clothes were a great deal like Alanna herself. Sleek, cool and sophisticated on the outside; soft, sexy, and so very, very hot on the inside.

"Have I told you today that you are beautiful?" His finger slipped a strap of the teddy down her arm.

The events of the past twenty-four hours dimmed as her head began to cloud. "I don't think so."

"An oversight." The other strap followed. "Because you are the most stunning woman I've ever known." The teddy was clinging to her breasts; only the slightest tug would send it shimmering down around her waist. "And the most desirable." His lips skimmed her warming flesh, his tongue cut a wide swath along her collarbone. "And the sexiest."

His hands were so gentle on her skin. So slow. Was there ever a man so patient? Beguiled, Alanna wrapped her arms around his neck and allowed herself to bask in the soft glow of sensations he was bringing her.

There was no hurry, no rush. Just a lingering pleasure. When his lips lingered at her throat, her pulse hummed. When his hands caressed her breast, her blood heated. And when he drew the warm, burgeoning flesh into his mouth, she felt a corresponding tug between her legs.

"Oh, Jonas." A soft moan escaped her lips. "I really do love you."

It was the answer he'd been waiting for. "I'm glad to hear that," he said. "Since I've no intention of letting you get away."

Alanna couldn't determine whether that was a promise or a threat. Before she could dwell upon it, the phone rang.

"Someone's got lousy timing," Jonas muttered.

"Are you expecting a call?"

"No one knows I'm here." They exchanged a long, knowing look, then biting back a curse, Jonas reached out and picked up the receiver. "Hello, Elizabeth."

There was a moment's hesitation. "Hello, Jonas," Elizabeth said. "How did you know it was me?"

"I guess I'm just getting psychic in my old age."

There was another brief pause, as Elizabeth seemed unable to determine his mood or her response.

"Is there any special reason for this call?" Jonas asked, frustrated as he felt Alanna retreat. She pulled the top of the teddy back into place, but the strawberry flush darkening the flesh above the black lace was still visible.

"I was hoping I'd find Alanna there," Elizabeth answered.

His body was turning frustratingly soft. Nothing could throw cold water onto passion like a chat with your fiancée's former mother-in-law, Jonas decided. "It's for you."

Drawing in a deep breath, Alanna took the receiver he offered. "Hello, Elizabeth. I was just filling Jonas in on Mitch's condition. And our plans.... No, not yet." Her quiet denial had Jonas looking at her sharply. "I know." Unable to meet his probing gaze, Alanna briefly closed her eyes. "I was just getting to it, Elizabeth, when we got a little off track."

At that, Jonas lifted a dark brow; Alanna felt the blush rise in her cheeks. "No, I promise, I'll tell him now. As soon as I hang up. Really." Forcing a confidence into her tone that she was a long way from feeling, Alanna said, "Good night, Elizabeth. I'll see you in the morning."

Jonas took the receiver from her and replaced it in the cradle. "Tell me what?"

"It's a little complicated."

"Contrary to popular belief, those of us who work with our hands are not entirely unable to understand the English language. You'll just have to go slowly. And use words with less than three syllables."

Unused to sarcasm from Jonas, Alanna realized exactly how badly she was handling this. "I'm sorry Elizabeth interrupted."

"I can deal with that." His usually velvet voice sounded unusually gritty, like a bald tire on a gravel road. "So, why don't you quit stalling and let me in on whatever it is that you've been afraid to tell me?"

She stood up, waiting until she could control both her words and her voice. "You can't come home with me, Jonas."

"Why not?" His narrowed eyes frosted in a way she'd never seen before. "Or need I ask?"

"It's not what you think," she protested, reaching for her discarded jacket. The glimpse of creamy breast as she bent to pick it up momentarily distracted him. Desire. Anger. Fear. He'd experienced them all before, but never at the same time. And he damn well didn't like it.

Alanna knew obstinacy when she saw it; she'd just never witnessed it in Jonas. On the contrary, she'd always thought him the calmest, most easygoing person she'd ever met. "You're not even going to attempt to understand, are you?"

Jonas folded his arms across his chest. "Try me."

"All right. After tomorrow's Rose Garden ceremony, Mitch is returning home to San Francisco."

"I figured as much. So, I suppose you want me to pretend we don't know one another on the flight back to the city?"

"It's a little more complicated than that."

"Now why doesn't that surprise me?"

She hated his curt tone, his coldness, the way he had distanced himself from her. "Jonas—"

"Just quit dragging this out, Alanna. And tell me what the hell you and Elizabeth have planned."

"Mitch is going to be staying in our house."

"*Ours*, as in yours and mine? Or *ours*, as in yours and Mitch's?"

She'd met Jonas only days after buying the house. They'd planned every aspect of the renovation together; it would always be as much Jonas's home as hers. Distressed by exactly how much his words stung and loath to show it, she crossed the room to where she'd left the key to the suite on the table by the door. "You know the answer to that."

Dread and frustration conspired to make his words rash. "I used to think I did. But that was before your husband returned from the dead."

"Former husband," Alanna murmured.

"I know that and you know that," he countered, covering the space between them in three long strides. "But when the hell is he going to find out that you are no longer Mrs. Mitchell Cantrell?"

He'd effectively trapped her between the table and himself. Alanna could feel his strength, although their bodies were barely touching. After last night she was not as surprised as she might once have been, that he could be every bit as fierce as he was gentle.

"I'll tell him soon," she promised. "As soon as he's recovered. And that's why I need you to take an earlier flight back and take all your things out of the house." The words tumbled out, as if Alanna were eager to get them out of the way. Not wanting to fight, she framed his scowling face in her hands. "You've been so wonderfully understanding about all this, Jonas. So patient. Just give me a bit more time. Please?"

Jonas damn well didn't feel understanding. Or patient. Crushing his mouth to hers, he kissed her with every bit of the pent-up anger he was feeling.

The kiss sent her reeling. Afraid that her knees were going to give way, Alanna clung to his shoulders and allowed the fire to blaze. Too soon, he released her. Still shaken, she stared up at him, letting him see the desire she knew was laced with confusion in her sea-green eyes.

"I want you to remember," he said. "How it feels. How we feel. Together." Passion, still unrelieved, thundered through him as he slid his hand under her jacket and caressed her tender breasts through the thin layer of silk.

Before she could answer, he opened the door. "You'd better go now, Alanna. Before I give in to my baser instincts and tie you to my bed. Where we both know you belong."

Shoving her out and into the hall, he firmly shut the door between them, leaving Alanna stunned. Wanting.

7

IT WAS TURNING OUT to be even more difficult than he'd imagined. Jonas had known that taking his things out of Alanna's house would be difficult. But he hadn't figured such a flood of emotions would hit the moment he entered the cheery, sunlit bedroom.

Here, in the room he'd finished first, Alanna had allowed her romantic side free rein. The morning fog had burned off, and the sun was shining through the sheer lace draperies, casting a warm, buttery glow across the room. The lacy, wrought iron bed, strewn with frilly pillows, held center stage, evoking sensual memories that were almost painful, given the circumstances of his visit today.

Shaking off what he considered self-defeating feelings, he quickly began opening dresser drawers, pulling out random pieces of underwear and sweaters and stuffing them haphazardly into the suitcase he'd brought with him. The closet was next. When he viewed Alanna's lace fantasy of a wedding dress, he debated leaving it right where it was. After all, he reasoned with a stab of unaccustomed bitterness, she'd only instructed him to remove *his* things from her house. She hadn't mentioned the dress. The idea that she hadn't mentioned it because she'd forgotten its existence was even more depressing than his reason for being here in the first place. If she could forget the dress so easily, did that mean that she could also forget him? Or what they had together?

"Don't be an idiot," he muttered, glaring at himself in the white-wicker-framed mirror that hung over a matching wicker dressing table strewn with white candles, silver-backed brushes, and her collection of crystal perfume atomizers. "The only reason she forgot the dress is because of all the pressure she's been under." Picking up one midnight-blue atomizer, he squeezed the gilded bulb. When the provocative, all too familiar scent called up an ache deep in his loins, he cursed softly.

He wasn't going to lose her, Jonas vowed as he stripped the closet of his clothes. As honestly sorry as he was about Mitch Cantrell's five-year nightmare, just because the guy had pulled off the miracle of the year, it didn't mean that he could pick up his life—and his wife—exactly as he'd left them. Alanna was Jonas's now. And he was damned if he was going to give her up without one hell of a fight.

After he finished packing, he stopped in the bedroom doorway for one long last look, flinching when his traitorous mind created a picture of Mitch and Alanna, spending a lazy Sunday morning in that lacy bed. The bed he and Alanna had bought together. Then an idea occurred to him. An idea so outrageous that he knew it could backfire, causing Alanna to be so furious with him that she might actually turn to Mitch in spite. *But what the hell*, Jonas figured, putting down his bag and rolling up his sleeves. It was worth the risk.

And besides, he reminded himself as he went to work, all was fair in love and war.

THE NEXT WEEK passed in a blur. Alanna knew that someday she'd wish she could remember the details; after all, how many times did one get the opportunity to meet the president? But lack of sleep and worry had fogged her mind so badly that she could only hope she had responded coherently to the president's warm remarks.

Despite Mitch's complaints, the Rose Garden ceremony had been postponed when his symptoms escalated, his first night in the hospital. After extensive tests revealed nothing more than a particularly debilitating virus, the ceremony was rescheduled, after which he was allowed to return home to San Francisco.

The medicine prescribed by the doctor had knocked Mitch out, causing him to sleep the entire flight home, which left Alanna alone with her turbulent thoughts. Elizabeth, seated across the aisle from her son, seemed no more eager for conversation than was she. A distancing was slowly growing between the two women who'd once been as close as mother and daughter. Because although they both had Mitch's welfare at heart, each had a different idea about exactly how to accomplish that. While Elizabeth hadn't said the words out loud, it was becoming increasingly apparent that she believed Alanna's place was with Mitch.

Mitch woke with a start when the wheels of the DC-10 hit the runway. "Allie?"

He grasped her hand so tightly that it took an effort not to cringe. "I'm here, Mitch. Everything's all right. We're just landing in San Francisco."

His vision still strangely glazed, he looked confusedly out the window at the scene that was at the same time both familiar and alien. "San Francisco? Not Beirut?"

"Not Beirut," she said quietly, exchanging a brief glance with Elizabeth across the aisle. "You must have been dreaming."

Hating the sympathy he viewed in Alanna's somber eyes, Mitch dragged his hand down his face. "I was. I was dreaming of that day." He tried to repress a shudder, as the vivid memory of his abduction and subsequent torture coursed through him.

With an effort Alanna did not weep at the terror that briefly swept across her former husband's face. Although Mitch had yet to share the details of his captivity with her, she'd always known what he'd gone through. Tales from released hostages had made her blood run cold. Closing her eyes against a new flood of pain, she pressed her forehead against his.

"It's all over, Mitch," she whispered, running her hands over his shoulders and down his arms. "You're safe. Back home in San Francisco."

"Home." Mitch drew in a deep, calming breath as he leaned back in his seat, vowing not to reveal any more lingering dread from the nightmare. The last thing he wanted was Allie's sympathy. "With my wife," he said. "My Allie." Giving her a long look fraught with emotion, he returned his gaze to the window as the airliner taxied to the terminal.

While Mitch drank in the sight of his beloved city, Alanna fumbled with the latch on her seat belt, steadfastly refusing to meet her mother-in-law's probing gaze.

They exited the ramp to the blinding glare of flashbulbs and a horde of reporters shouting questions. While Mitch stood at the gate and read the brief, carefully prepared statement that had been cleared ahead of time by the State Department, Alanna wondered how they'd ever escape the crush of people. Just when she was afraid they'd be there all day, an airport security guard appeared at her elbow, informing her that her brother was waiting for them in a private lounge adjoining the gate.

"I'm sorry," she interrupted, when Mitch began fielding questions, "but my husband has had a grueling experience, and he's not well. He's made his statement. That's all for today."

When Mitch looked inclined to argue, she shifted her carry-on bag to the other shoulder, took hold of his arm and practically dragged him through the complaining throng, escaping into the lounge the guard had indicated. She had never been so glad to see anyone as she was to see her older brother.

"Oh, David," she murmured, wrapping her arms around him, "I'm so glad you're here."

"I'm just sorry I was out of the country when all this went down," David Fairfield said. "But Jonas has filled me in."

Alanna tilted her head. "How is he?" she asked softly.

Viewing the dark purple circles under her eyes, David didn't know whom he felt sorrier for. "He's been better," he said under his breath. Knowing that this was neither the time nor the place for such a personal conversation, he turned toward Mitch. "Well, hail the conquering hero." David held out his hand.

"Hardly a hero," Mitch muttered, shaking hands with his brother-in-law.

"That's not what I read in the *Chronicle*," David countered. "You're looking great, Mitch," he said with false heartiness. "Really great."

Mitch's grin was the first real smile Alanna had viewed all day. "Spoken like a true lawyer. And although we both know that's rubbish, thanks for the vote of confidence."

That same deep voice that had brought the news into living rooms from all the world's hot spots lacked its usual resonance. David's expression sobered. "So how are you really?"

Alanna broke in before Mitch had a chance to answer. "Mitch has a slight bug. But the doctor assured us that with the proper medication and a little bed rest, he'll soon be as good as new. Isn't that right, Mitch?"

Again Mitch opened his mouth to respond, but Alanna was quicker. "And rather than keep him on his feet any longer than necessary, Elizabeth, why don't you take Mitch out to the car, while David and I retrieve the luggage? David, tell Elizabeth where the car is parked."

He'd no sooner given her the location, when Alanna turned to the airport security officer and requested a wheelchair.

"I'm perfectly capable of walking, Allie," Mitch complained.

"Of course you are, Mitch," she said agreeably. "But don't forget, you nearly fainted during your meeting with the president."

"I only got a little light-headed for a moment," Mitch insisted. "Besides, it wasn't really a meeting," he tacked on with a flare of his old strength. "It was a photo op, a grip and grin for the returning so-called hero."

It had taken less than a week of marriage to Mitchell Cantrell to learn that cynicism was a way of life in the press corps. And while Mitch's attitude had once upset her, now Alanna found his swift return to character encouraging. "Whatever it was, it still wore you out," she said. "For heaven's sake, after what you've been through, it's amazing that you were able to survive that media zoo. So, for your own good, I'm going to insist that you follow my advice."

Advice? How about orders? Mitch wondered when Allie had gotten so bossy. Recognizing intransigence when he saw it, he suggested, "How about we cut a deal?"

"What kind of deal?"

"You forget the wheelchair and I'll meekly go along with Mom and wait in the car, while you and David retrieve our luggage."

Alanna knew that was the closest she'd get to an admission that the day had taken its toll on him. "You're on."

Minutes later she was standing with her brother at the luggage carousel. "How is he really?" David asked again.

"I don't know. The doctor assured us that the virus isn't dangerous, but I still can't help worrying about more long-term effects."

David studied her face minutely. "I take it you haven't told him about Jonas."

"I haven't had a chance."

"But you will."

Alanna's fingers tightened on the strap of her flight bag. "Of course. There's one," she said, pointing out the approaching gray suitcase.

David plucked it off the conveyor belt. "When?"

"As soon as the time is right."

"The longer you wait, the harder it's going to be."

"Now that sounds familiar," Alanna complained peevishly. "Did Jonas send you here to cross-examine me?"

"You should know better than that. I'm your big brother. It's only natural that I'd be worried about you."

"You're also Jonas's best friend."

"You make it sound like something I should apologize for."

"Don't be ridiculous. I think that's Elizabeth's." Alanna pointed out another suitcase.

David checked the number on the tag looped around the handle against the one Elizabeth had handed him, then retrieved the case. "Any more?"

"No. There were only those two cases. Mitch didn't have that much. All his things fitted into my luggage." As they walked out of the terminal, the wind coming off the Bay whipped at Alanna's hair, blowing it into her eyes, but she appeared not to notice. "Have you spoken with Jonas recently?"

"We had a couple of beers together last night." David decided not to mention how he and Jonas had spent the past week. After all, he decided pragmatically, Alanna would find out for herself, soon enough. And although he'd totally understood Jonas's motivation, David had no intention of being caught in the fallout.

"How is he?"

"Think about it for a minute," David suggested. "How would you feel if the situation were reversed? If three weeks before your wedding, Jonas's wife suddenly appeared on the scene?"

"Jonas doesn't have a wife."

"Moot point," he said mildly as they waited for an Airporter bus to pass before crossing to the parking garage. "You're an imaginative woman, Alanna. How would you feel, if you were in Jonas's place?"

Since she'd thought of little else the entire flight home, the answer came instantly. "I'd be miserable. And angry. And probably scared, as well."

David nodded, satisfied. "I rest my case."

She stopped and looked up at him. "I do love Jonas, David. And Mitch coming back hasn't changed that. Really," she insisted, when he lifted a challenging dark brow. "But you have to help me make him understand that I just need a little more time."

"Mitch has always been a staunch advocate of the truth, Alanna. He's built his career on it. How do you think he's going to feel when he discovers you've been lying to him?"

"I'm not lying."

The sharp look he gave her had always worked wonders during cross-examination. When faced with that unwavering stare, more than one witness had caved in under the pressure. It was, Alanna realized suddenly, the same probing look that Mitch had perfected.

"You also aren't telling him the truth. Lies of omission hurt just the same when they're ultimately discovered, kiddo." His firm look gave way to sympathy. "Mitch is one tough guy, Sis. If he could get through the past five years, he'll be able to accept the fact that you've built yourself a new life."

One that didn't include him, Alanna considered as they approached David's car. When she viewed Mitch looking strangely lonely in the back seat, she could only hope that her brother was right.

ALONE AT LAST, Mitch thought. After innumerable cups of Earl Grey tea and shortbread cookies Alanna had retrieved from the freezer, Elizabeth finally asked David to take her home. Alanna had walked them out to the car, leaving Mitch free to catch his breath.

He'd forgotten how fast everyone spoke. And all at once. Ever since he'd arrived at the air force base in Wiesbaden, people had been shooting words at him like bullets, expecting the proper responses in return. He suspected that he'd talked more in the past week and a half than he had in the last year, and the effort to keep up his end of the conversation was becoming increasingly wearying.

Finishing off the lukewarm tea, he pushed himself out of the bentwood rocker and began roaming the kitchen. The room, with its wood-burning stove and creamy-white paint highlighted by an expanse of stained wood, exuded an old-world charm. His gaze took in the small, hexagonal, blue-and-white-tiled countertops, the etched glass cabinet inserts, the antique pub clock hanging on the wall beside a collection of butter molds fashioned from copper, pewter, wood and earthenware. It was a room that brought to mind just-baked bread, Devon cream, fresh eggs. And although he'd never been here before, despite the fact that it was certainly not the type of room he'd ever thought of living in, Mitch understood why the phrase "Home, Sweet Home" had been coined by the Victorians.

He paused in front of an eye-catching assortment of blue-and-white Victorian china displayed on the shelves of a corner hutch, and was examining a platter when Alanna returned.

"You must be exhausted," she said. Her grave eyes scanned his face for lingering traces of fever. "I thought they'd never leave."

"I'm fine," he said, not quite truthfully. Although some maniac was still pounding away in his head with a sledgehammer, Mitch was getting extremely tired of the way Allie kept walking around him, as if on eggshells. In his fantasies—those vivid images that had kept him sane for five long years—her emerald-green eyes had blazed with passion, not pity, when she looked up at him.

"Still—"

"This is quite a collection you've acquired," he interrupted, anxious to change the subject to anything other than his health, which, he reluctantly had to admit, wasn't what he'd like it to be. Even if Allie would agree to go upstairs to bed with him, which he strongly doubted, he probably wouldn't be able to deliver. "Did you find it all in one place?"

"Hardly." Allie thought of all the garage sales she and Jonas had attended up and down the California coast, all the way from Monterey to Marin County. "Actually, it's been like a treasure hunt. It's amazing the stuff people have stashed away in their attics. If you're lucky, some of it can be had for a song."

"Still," Mitch mused, looking around, "this extensive renovation can't come cheap."

Alanna followed his gaze to the sun room that Jonas had convinced her to build, the room that most harkened back to the Victorians' love of nature. The walls of the sun-filled room were white-paned glass, the furniture a delicate white wicker. Lacy ferns nested in vintage brass containers, along with potted palms and shiny green ivy. An old tin milk bucket held a fragrant spray of fresh-cut flowers that Alanna knew had been Jonas's contribution to her homecoming.

"Don't forget, I do have my grandmother's trust fund," she reminded him. "And although it isn't that large, I was lucky to have found a contractor willing to work within my budget. Besides, my job at the magazine pays a great deal more than lecturing at the university."

"It should. If this afternoon's phone calls are any indication, you're working twice as hard." Mitch had lost count of the number of times the phone had rung in the past hour and a half, all professed emergencies that needed his wife's guiding hand. "It makes me wonder how your aunt was able to put her precious magazine out before you came on board."

Alanna thought she detected a note of sarcasm in his tone, but opted not to comment on it. "*San Francisco Trends* is a very good magazine, and I'm proud that Aunt Marian chose me to be special features editor," she said mildly.

The rebuff was polite, but Mitch got her message. Loud and clear. "She's lucky to have you. And I can't wait to read it."

Alanna wondered why Mitch's professional approval was suddenly so important to her. Perhaps because he was a journalistic legend, while she was still a novice. "It's not exactly the *New Yorker*," she said. "But we like to think it manages to inform the public, while entertaining them at the same time."

For the first time since their stilted reunion, Mitch got a sense of the old Allie. Sensing her unspoken need for approval, he said, "I always knew that you'd be a whiz at whatever you chose to do, sweetheart."

Alanna hated the way his simply spoken compliment gave her such undeniable pleasure. "I'd better show you to your room." She was headed toward the spiral staircase when the phone rang again.

"Go answer it." Mitch bit back his frustration. "I'll get settled in, while you tend to business. Just point the way."

"It's the first door on the right," she said. "You can't miss it. It's the only bedroom that's not in a state of chaos."

Directions given, she answered the telephone. "Yes, Marian," Mitch heard her say. "Yes, Brandon assured me that he'd send the photos by courier, no later than the end of the week. Yes, I've already received the article and sent it down to copyediting. Yes, that's all taken care of."

Her tone was brisk, confident, totally in control. Once again Mitch felt oddly disoriented, alone in this strange house with a woman he couldn't quite recognize. Although he told himself that he should not have expected the world to stop spinning during his time in captivity, he couldn't help experiencing a vague feeling of resentment at the way life—most particularly Alanna's life—had so successfully continued without him. Heaving a weary sigh, he climbed the rest of the way up the stairs, stopping in front of the door Alanna had indicated.

Alanna found him still standing in the doorway nearly five minutes later. "Mitch? Is anything wrong?"

"I think I must have misunderstood you."

Alanna stared into her bedroom, unable to believe her eyes. The white iron bed had been dismantled; parts of it were propped against bare plaster walls. The wallpaper had disappeared, as had the curtains and all of the furniture. Sawdust littered the stenciled oak floor, and the electric wall sconces dangled from bare red and black wires. Five-gallon cans of paint claimed the corner where her wicker dressing table had been, while piles of new plasterboard took up the center of the room.

"Damn you, Jonas Harte," she muttered under her breath, vowing to kill him the moment she could lay her hands on him. It was one thing to be jealous of her former husband's return; that she could understand. Even accept. But to destroy her lovely bedroom, just to keep Mitch from sleeping in her bed, was too much! Fuming, she marched into the adjoining bathroom, relieved to find it untouched.

"Who's Jonas Harte?" Mitch asked when she rejoined him.

"Mr. Harte is my contractor," she said through gritted teeth, while trying to get control of her escalating blood pressure. "He assured me the room would be ready for you when we got home."

Mitch's skeptical gaze circled the debacle. "I don't know anything about construction, Allie," he said slowly, "but I'd say the man would have to be a miracle worker to get this mess cleaned up before the turn of the century."

"Oh, you'd be surprised what Jonas can do when he puts his mind to it," Alanna countered dryly. Breathing a long sigh born of frustration, she added, "I suppose we have no choice but to put you in the old nursery. But I have to warn you, it's rather dreary. And the roof leaks when it rains."

"Don't worry about it. I've gotten used to dreary."

His matter-of-fact attitude sent a stab of guilt through her. What kind of selfish person was she to be so angry about the mere destruction of a room when Mitch had had his entire life destroyed? Well, five years of it, Alanna amended as she led him down the hall.

"Still," she went on, "I wish I could have had everything ready for you. As it is, I'm afraid this is the best I can do, although . . ." Words failed her, as she stared at the room that had been in a state of total disrepair when she'd left for Washington.

Now the walls were a mottled sand color, the ceiling a soothing sky blue. The brass bed—a single, Alanna noted—was covered with the fluffy, yellow-and-white goose down quilt she'd admired last month in an antique store. The remainder of the furnishings had been kept simple: a bamboo table beside the bed, a nineteenth-century trunk at the foot, a folding screen in a corner, a mahogany four-drawer chest against one wall. Goose-neck reading lamps were attached to the wall, balloon shades had been hung at the arched windows, a needle-point rug covered the floor.

"It's lovely," Mitch said, joining her in the doorway.

"Yes, it is, isn't it?"

Mitch looked at her curiously. "You sound surprised."

Surprised was putting it mildly. Alanna shook her head, wondering how Jonas had managed to practically demolish one perfect room and still put this one together in one short week.

"It's only been recently finished," she hedged. "In a way, I almost feel as if I'm seeing it for the first time."

Mitch entered the room, running his finger along the delicate rosettes carved into the chair rail that divided the wall. "Did your contractor do this detail work?"

"He does it in his spare time," she said. "Wood carving was always his hobby."

"He's quite talented."

"Yes. He is."

Mitch rocked back and forth on his heels as he looked around the room. Although he'd never been interested in doing things with his hands, he had always admired anyone who worked to perfect his craft, whatever it was. "I'm looking forward to meeting him."

Tell him, the little voice in the back of Alanna's mind urged. *Tell him now.* Alanna ignored it. "He'll be here in the morning. I'll introduce you then."

"I'd like that." Mitch was studying the walls, intrigued by the way the paint had been mottled. The person who'd done the job was clearly an artisan, who took obvious pride in his work. "I have a feeling that he and I have a lot in common."

Oh, Mitch, Alanna thought miserably. *If you only knew.* "Let me help you get settled," she said instead, inwardly damning herself for being such a coward. She went out to the hall linen closet and retrieved a handful of fluffy yellow towels. "You'll have to use the bathroom adjoining the larger bedroom. It's the only one on this floor that works."

Mitch looked skeptical. "Not that I'm all that choosy, Allie, but I hope, for your sake, that it's in better condition than the bedroom. I'd hate to think of you forced to take baths in the kitchen sink."

"It was the first room I had Jonas, uh, Mr. Harte, do," she assured him. "Believe me, there's plenty of hot water and the toilet no longer runs all day and night."

"There were times that any running water would have seemed a treat."

A very strong part of Alanna—the guilty part—didn't want to know what Mitch had suffered. Another, more rational part, knew she could not go through life with her head buried in the sand, simply because it might prove less painful.

"We need to talk about it," she said softly. "About what happened."

Mitch nodded. "I know. But not now."

Her relief was patent. "No," she agreed. "Not now." She began turning down the bed. "Why don't you go take a long, hot bath?" she suggested. "And I'll go downstairs and warm you some milk."

"Allie. Sweetheart." Mitch caught her arm on her way out the door. "I'm your husband, not a helpless infant. I don't need any warm milk."

"I'm sorry. I just thought it might relax you."

He ran his palm down her hair. "Being home with you is all the relaxation I need." Or it would be, Mitch considered, if she weren't so damn tense. Although he tried to tell himself that it was only his overactive imagination, he could have sworn that she almost flinched when he touched her. "May I ask a question?"

"Of course." He was suddenly so close. Too close.

Her polite little smile tied his stomach in knots. "Where are you going to sleep?"

She glanced at the bed, a bed that was obviously not meant for two. *Cute, Jonas,* she thought grimly. *And decidedly obvious.* "No problem," she assured Mitch. "There's a lounge in the parlor. I can sleep on it."

"You could." Her skin looked as soft as satin. Unable to resist, Mitch trailed his knuckles down the side of her face. "Or you could stay up here with me." His thumb traced the outline of her upper lip. "The bed may be narrow, but we could always find a way to make room. Remember our honeymoon? When we slept like spoons nestled in a drawer?"

Her lips parted instinctively at his tender touch, even as her mind warned her that things were definitely on the verge of getting out of hand. *Tell him!* the voice of reason screamed yet again. Again, Alanna could not quite find the words.

"I don't remember us sleeping much at all that night," she said instead.

He smiled reminiscently. "You're right. It must have been the next night, on the plane." His voice had taken on a soft, intimate tone that caused color to flame in her cheeks as she thought back to that long, overseas flight. Although she'd never honestly believed it possible to actually make love undetected on an airplane, Mitch had proved her wrong.

"Allie?"

"Oh, Mitch."

They both spoke at once. "You first," she said.

"I thought it would be easier," he admitted. His gaze moved over her face, lingering on each feature as he thought how he used to love to watch her face as he took her over the top. "I thought we'd be easier together."

Torn with guilt, Alanna held herself very still. "It's been a long time, Mitch. Things have changed. We've changed."

"Are you saying that you just need a little time to get used to the idea of me being around?" He reached out and took her hand in both of his, carefully watching her face as he tried to rub some warmth into her icy fingers.

Alanna's heartbeat was like a hammer in her chest as she tried to rein in her runaway emotions. Sensual memories stirred by Mitch's touch warred with thoughts of Jonas. And of the life they'd built together.

"Gracious," she said suddenly, her eyes darting to the antique clock hanging on the wall. She'd been looking for one for months; where on earth had Jonas found it? "Look at the time. You must be absolutely exhausted."

Mitch's fingers tightened, effectively holding her hostage. "Not too tired to discuss whatever it is that has you acting so damn jumpy." A thought suddenly occurred to him. A thought so unpalatable, he feared he might lose the light supper he'd eaten on the airplane. He narrowed his eyes. "Perhaps I've been taking too much for granted," he said slowly, deliberately, as he tried to make sense of his whirling thoughts. "You correctly stated that we'd both changed. Are you trying to tell me that you no longer have any feelings for me, Allie? Is that it?"

Here's your opening, the nagging little voice pointed out. *Go for it.* "Oh, Mitch." Alanna exhaled a sad little sigh and placed her free hand, the one he wasn't practically crushing, against his cheek. His beard was rough against her fingertips, reminding her of how it had once felt against her skin, after he'd returned home from days in forbidden territories. "Of course I still have feelings for you," she said truthfully. "How could I not?"

The guilt she'd experienced earlier was nothing like that which gripped her heart when he gave her a crookedly boyish, obviously relieved smile.

"I guess I'm just overanalyzing things." Bending his head, he brushed his lips against her cheek. "In case I'm contagious," he said at her surprised look when he avoided her mouth. "I'd hate for you to come down with whatever this is, just when I'm getting better."

"It would be pretty bad timing," Alanna agreed, thinking of all the work piled up on her desk.

"You're telling me. It's bad enough having to put off our reunion, while we wait for me to shake this damn bug." He gave her a slow, sexy wink. "Although the idea of keeping you in bed for days on end is decidedly appealing, I'd rather you be at full strength for the celebration I intend to have, as soon as I get back on my feet."

Cheered by the demonstration that his wife's feelings hadn't changed during his absence, that she still loved him, Mitch scooped up the sunshine-yellow towels from the bed and went down the hall to the bathroom. He was whistling.

Emotionally drained, Alanna slumped onto the single bed, put her face into her hands and silently wept.

8

ALTHOUGH ALANNA KNEW she was being a coward, she was admittedly relieved when Mitch opted to sleep in the following morning. Gulping down a quick cup of coffee and a high-protein, high-fiber breakfast bar, she left him a cheery note, giving him her office number. Dithering uncharacteristically over exactly how to sign the brief note, she finally opted for a simple initial A.

From the moment she entered the office building in the Montgomery Street high rise, Alanna found herself too busy to dwell on her personal dilemma. Her secretary Karin, a young editorial assistant, greeted her with obvious relief.

"Am I ever glad you're back," she said, handing Alanna a thick stack of messages written on four colors of paper. "Things have been an absolute madhouse around here."

The blue notes were personal calls, white were business, yellow were pressing business issues and red were emergencies. Ever since Karin's arrival, Alanna's entire office had been color-coded, and although it had taken her a while to become accustomed to the vivid folders that had taken the place of the old familiar manila ones in her In basket, she had to admit that Karin was a paragon of organization; her system kept things running smoothly. In fact, Alanna considered, she'd never seen Karin look the slightest bit flustered—until today. "I take it we've got problems?"

"That's putting it mildly," Karin countered. "In fact, if those windows weren't sealed shut, half the staff probably would have jumped out four days ago." As if suddenly remembering the reason for Alanna's absence, she grimaced. "I'm sorry. I can't believe I could be so insensitive. That just shows you how crazy everything's been around here. So..." She took a deep breath and gave Alanna a sympathetic look. "How is Mitch? And more importantly, how are you?"

Good question, Alanna considered, wishing she knew the answer. "Other than a nasty virus, Mitch is fine. As for me, let's just say things are a little complicated right now."

"I can imagine." The eyes behind Karin's red-framed glasses revealed curiosity. A curiosity Alanna ignored.

"What's going on that has everyone so suicidal?"

"Marian didn't tell you?"

"I've been a little preoccupied lately," Alanna said dryly. "Tell me what?"

"That Ramsey Tremayne is trying to take over *San Francisco Trends*."

Ramsey Tremayne was a brash Australian millionaire who'd been gobbling up magazines and newspapers as if he were starving, and who viewed the American publishing establishment as his own personal smorgasbord. "You can't be serious."

"It's true." Karin didn't bother to hide her disdain. "I didn't graduate with honors to work for Flash and Trash Tremayne."

"But we're not his type of publication," Alanna pointed out. "So what would he want with us?"

"You'll have to ask Marian that," Karin said. "She's waiting for you in her office. I promised to send you in as soon as you arrived. Oh, and Jonas called just before you got here, to remind you that today's the day you're supposed to pick out the tile for the downstairs bathroom. He said he'll meet you at the shop at noon."

"I'm probably going to have to cancel that," Alanna replied, looking down at the stack of messages. "Would you do me a favor and call him back and tell him we'll have to reschedule?"

"Sure." Again Karin's eyes asked questions. Again, Alanna ignored them.

"I'll be in Marian's office, if anyone calls."

As Alanna walked down the long hallway toward her aunt's office, she decided that at least this new crisis with Ramsey Tremayne would take her mind off her personal problems. If only for a while.

MITCH WOKE to the sound of pounding. At first his sleep-hazed mind thought he was locked in a building that was being shelled, but gradually, as he took in the cozy room, he remembered that he was not in Beirut at all, but San Francisco. In Allie's home.

Allie. Home. Had any two words ever sounded so sweet? Tugging on the jeans Alanna had bought for him in Washington, he went looking for the source of the steady repetitive noise.

He located the workman on the first floor of the house, nailing wallboard over the exposed studs in the room he remembered Allie describing as the back parlor. The room that was being converted into a combination library and office.

He watched for a while, marveling at the way the man's hammer never once missed the mark. Had it been him, Mitch mused, he would have smashed his thumb at least a dozen times. He cleared his throat. "Would you be Jonas Harte?"

Jonas stiffened. Neck, shoulders, arms, back. Lowering the hammer, he turned, coming face-to-face with Mitch's approving smile. It was the same face he'd watched for years on television. But strangely different, Jonas decided. It was as if the experiences of the past years had added maturity, rather than age, to the newsman's handsome features, making them even more appealing, if that were possible. With an icy stab of jealousy, Jonas wondered if Alanna had found the guy more appealing. More desirable.

"That's me. And you're . . ."

"Mitch Cantrell. Alanna's husband," Mitch divulged, not knowing how badly those innocent words hurt. "My wife's right, Mr. Harte. You're very good. Your craftsmanship in the upstairs bedroom is exceptional."

"Thanks." He searched Mitch's face for some sign as to exactly what Alanna had told her husband. *Former husband*, he reminded himself. "But it helps to have a discriminating client who knows exactly what she wants." At least she used to, Jonas tacked on silently. Until you showed up.

Mitch rubbed his unshaven chin as he looked around the room. Plaster dust was everywhere, floating on the morning sunbeams. "It's funny, thinking of Allie that way," he murmured.

Jonas lifted a brow, but remained silent.

Mitch wandered over to a pair of sawhorses and stared down at the incomprehensible blueprints. "She mentioned that when you started, the house was in a shambles. That it's been more of a renovation than a simple remodeling job."

"The house sat empty for a long time. It needed a new foundation, roof, wiring, plumbing, the works."

Mitch shook his head in amazement. "She probably could have bought a luxury high-rise apartment for what this is costing her."

"I suppose so," Jonas agreed. "But she wanted this house."

His stony expression could have been carved onto the side of Mount Rushmore, Mitch thought. Wondering if he'd somehow offended Alanna's contractor, the newsman flashed one of his world-famous smiles. "It's only too bad she might have to leave it, before you get it finished."

"She hasn't said anything to me about leaving."

Mitch decided the contractor's warning expression stemmed from fear that he'd end up not being paid to complete the job. "Oh, nothing's been decided yet," he assured Jonas. "I haven't been home long enough to think about the future. But whatever happens, Mr. Harte, I guarantee that we'll meet the terms of your agreement with Alanna." That little detail taken care of, Mitch left the room, headed for the kitchen.

Left alone in the room that Alanna had insisted on turning into his office, and worried about the future, Jonas remembered the first day they'd met.

ALTHOUGH HE'D SEEN Alanna Cantrell innumerable times on television, the cameras hadn't done the woman justice, Jonas realized when she opened the door to his brisk knock. The door bell wasn't working.

Her warm, welcoming smile called up an involuntary sexual tug. "Please tell me that you're the wizard my brother sent to rescue me from all this."

"I'm Jonas Harte. But despite your brother's glowing reviews, I'm hardly a wizard." He glanced around at the exterior of a house that had definitely seen better days. The yard was overgrown, the paint was peeling, and all the downstairs windows were boarded up. "Although quite honestly, Mrs. Cantrell, I think you may need a helluva lot more than a wizard before this job is through."

"Don't tell me that you're a coward, Mr. Harte?" It was her eyes that made her beautiful, Jonas decided. They were so alive, so filled with intelligence and enthusiasm.

"No. But I am a realist, Mrs. Cantrell. And I've seen too many people rush into buying one of these quaint old Victorians, with the idea that a few weekends with a paintbrush and lawn mower is all they'll have to invest, before they're sitting on their front porch enjoying a glass of ice-cold lemonade."

"I realized from the start that this project was going to be more difficult than that," Alanna countered calmly. "The inspection report was quite thorough."

"You've gotten an inspection report?"

"Of course. And although the conclusion was admittedly less than encouraging, I knew from the moment I saw the magnificent view of the Bay from the upstairs bedroom that I simply had to have this house, whatever the final appraisal."

A romantic, Jonas decided. He should have figured as much. Who else but a romantic would dream of owning a gingerbread-encrusted, Victorian home in the first place? And who else but another romantic would give up a thriving architectural career to renovate them? he asked himself honestly.

"Well, let's see what we're talking about," he said.

Thirty minutes later, he was shaking his head as he studied the inspector's report. "Have you considered just tearing the place down and starting over?"

Her answer was direct and to the point. "No."

"It'd probably be easier. And cheaper."

"Money's no problem, within reason," she responded easily. "My grandmother left me a generous trust fund that's been quietly compiling interest for the past twenty years."

"Perhaps you should be more careful about revealing that financial information," Jonas warned. "There are a lot of contractors out there who'd add on an additional fifty to eighty percent if they thought they could get away with it."

He saw Alanna give his face a quick study, appearing satisfied with what she saw. "But not you."

"No," Jonas agreed. "Not me."

This time her smile reached her eyes, brightening them to a warm, inviting emerald. "So, now that you've seen the worst—" she gestured toward the lengthy report "—how about my giving you the grand tour?"

Forewarned by the report, Jonas told himself that he shouldn't have been surprised by the condition of the rambling house. But he was. Because closer examination showed it to be even worse than the preliminary inspection had indicated. Alanna's beloved house was, to put it charitably, a mess. He was trying to decide exactly how to suggest that she cut her losses and find another more practical house to buy, when she led him into an upstairs room.

"It's incredible." He crossed the room to the narrow arched window that was much too small for such a dazzling view. The setting sun had gilded the waters of the Bay a gleaming gold; white sails fluttered gaily in the wind, sea gulls skimmed low on the waters, searching for fish. He stood there, his gaze captured by a trio of dark shapes, moving like shadows through the water.

"Are those what I think they are?"

"Whales," Alanna acknowledged, awe evident in a voice that was half honey, half smoke. "Aren't they incredible?" A momentary fantasy of that sultry voice murmuring his name, while making love, flashed through his mind, calling forth yet another stir of desire. This one more powerful than the first.

She was standing beside him, watching the migrating whales cut a determined dark swath through the golden path of water. She looked up at him. "So, what do you think?"

What do I think? That you have incredible eyes. The kind a man could stare into for hours. "About the whales?" Jonas asked.

A question appeared in her eyes. "About the house."

"Oh." It took an effort, but Jonas returned his mind to his reason for coming here today. "Well, to begin with, your foundation's dying."

"Please tell me that isn't as bad as it sounds."

"It's not good. Most of these old Victorians were erected on cedar posts, because portland cement was just being introduced and masons were expensive. And although cedar is decay resistant and lasts indefinitely in our climate, yours has suffered some termite damage."

"Can't we just call in an exterminator?"

"Sure. You'd want to do that, anyway. But you'll have another problem, when you try to get financing. Most banks these days require concrete foundations."

"Are you saying I won't be able to get a loan?"

"Probably not until you replace the foundation."

"And what exactly does that entail?"

Jonas began sketching on the legal pad he'd been using for taking notes. "First we jack up the building, so the old beams and posts can be pulled out. Then we dig perimeter trenches and forms for footings and walls. Concrete is poured into the forms, which, depending on the weather, should cure in a couple of days. Then the house is lowered onto its new foundation and bolted to the concrete."

Alanna studied the drawings for a long, silent moment. "All right. What else?"

"You'll need a new roof. Previous owners have put about three layers of asphalt shingles on top of the original wood, which have put a lot of weight on the roof support structure. One good windstorm could do it in. I'd suggest removing all the old materials, repairing any structural damage, and beginning again with new cedar shingles. That way the roof will look authentic, add more value to your house and should, in our climate, last for a lifetime."

"I like the idea of permanency," Alanna said. Although a very strong part of her had been yearning for a house of her own since the early days of her marriage, lately her nesting instincts seemed to have grown even stronger. "So, a new foundation and a new roof. What else?"

"This old iron plumbing is a ticking bomb. You'll need copper."

"I suspected as much from the inspection report. What about the bathtub? Please tell me we can save it."

As Jonas considered the old lion-footed tub, a sudden, provocative image of Alanna, up to her chin in frothy white bubbles, flashed through his mind. "The tub's a goner. But don't worry. I know where you can get your hands on a great old copper one that'll be even better."

"It sounds wonderful," Alanna agreed. "Is that it?" she asked hopefully.

"Not yet. You're just asking for a fire with that hodgepodge of wiring. The common thing with these old houses is that each new owner adds on some more power, resulting in a mess of different wiring styles, all adding up to an inadequate supply at the main switch. Your best bet is to replace it all."

"New wiring."

"Along with new walls, since you'll obviously decide to change some of the interior layout."

"Gracious," Alanna said weakly. "I knew it was going to be a challenge, but I never imagined I was taking on a lifetime project."

"I told you it wasn't going to be easy," Jonas reminded her. "But so long as you know what you want, and understand what to expect, we should be able to get it done with only a few minor glitches, rather than a major disaster."

"You said we. Does that mean you'll take the job?"

"I suppose it does. If you're still determined to go through with it."

Alanna's gaze shifted briefly out the window, before returning to Jonas. From the look in her eyes, he knew that she truly loved this house. And she was determined to live here, whatever it took.

"I never could resist a challenge," she said. "So, before you change your mind, why don't you let me buy you a drink at the pub down the street to celebrate our collaboration?"

He wondered if there was a man alive who could say no to those eyes. "You've got yourself a deal. But I'm buying." When she looked inclined to argue the point, he said, "You'll need to save your money for the house."

She appeared to consider that for a moment. "All right. But next time it's my turn."

Jonas found that he liked the idea of a next time. "You're the boss," he said simply.

The Irish pub was small and intimate, with a beamed ceiling, heavy furniture, and a bartender who sounded as if he'd just come over on the boat from the auld sod. At this time of day the place was practically deserted; besides the bartender, the only other clientele was a pair of elderly men engaged in a lively game of darts.

Jonas and Alanna settled into a booth in the back of the pub. His mind already filled with plans, Jonas filled napkin after napkin with sketches. They'd have to replace that small window in her bedroom. Let in the magnificent view. And she should add a sun room onto the kitchen. A bright, cheery room filled with plants, a place that would serve as a retreat after a long week's work.

After an initial worry about maintaining the integrity of the original floor plan, Alanna enthusiastically accepted all his ideas, even adding a few of her own. When she leaned over to sketch an island counter in the center of the kitchen he'd drawn, Jonas drank in her scent, a rich, dark, complex perfume that reminded him of Paris. Of sultry, moon-spangled evenings, cool jazz and hot sex. Although he'd never before been tempted to mix work with pleasure, Jonas vowed that before this job was completed, he and Alanna Cantrell would be lovers.

"To the house," Alanna said, lifting her glass in a toast. Jonas found her smile every bit as stunning as her scent.

"To the house. And new challenges," he agreed.

NOW, as Jonas went back to work, he knew that he'd begun falling in love with her that very first day. When the renovation became a joint venture over the ensuing months, he realized that he couldn't remember a life without her. And couldn't picture a future without her in it.

They belonged together, he considered, swinging the hammer with renewed vigor. They were a team. And although he honestly sympathized with Alanna's plight, he knew he wasn't going to be able to relax until Mitchell Cantrell was out of this house. *Their house.*

MARIAN BURTON-WHITE was pacing a path in the lush carpeting of her executive office. "I've worked too hard to let that unprincipled Australian raider steal this magazine," she swore, lighting yet another cigarette, ignoring the one already burning in the ashtray.

Alanna reread her aunt's letter. "He doesn't say he's interested in tendering an offer," she pointed out.

"Why else would he want to meet with me?" Marian shot back.

"Perhaps his motive is as simple as he says," Alanna suggested. "He's coming to town next week and wants to take a fellow publisher to dinner."

"And pigs will fly. He's sniffing around, looking for the soft spot. I just know it."

"He won't find one," Alanna said confidently. Her aunt ran the tightest ship in the publishing business. "Besides, he can't buy what you refuse to sell."

"That's probably what the *Herald*'s publisher said, too," Marian retorted. "And Tremayne's name popped up on that masthead, just last week."

"I won't deny that he's been busy, but don't you think you're borrowing trouble?"

Puzzled, Alanna studied the older woman carefully. Never had she seen her aunt so flustered. Her silver-blond hair was atypically tousled from nervous fingers having run through it, her lipstick was chewed off, and her normally golden complexion, tanned from weekend sailing on the Bay, was strangely pale, save for the scarlet flags waving in her cheeks. Marian Burton-White had always been the epitome of competence. Something definitely had her disturbed, Alanna decided. Something more than a perceived takeover threat.

"Hah!" Marian smoked furiously as she paced the floor. "You don't have to borrow trouble when you're dealing with Ramsey Tremayne. He'll supply more than you need."

"You sound as if you know him."

Marian muttered something that could have been agreement or denial.

"I know," she said, turning around and fixing Alanna with a bright, feigned smile. "Ramsey's always had an eye for the ladies. Why don't you go to dinner with him? You can smile at him, charm him, then send him on his way." Her eyes hardened again. "Back to Australia. Where he belongs."

"My life's hectic enough right now," Alanna protested. "Besides, from the tone of his letter, it's clear that it's you he wants to meet with."

"Perhaps it's time Ramsey Tremayne learned that he can't always get what he wants," Marian said, more to herself than to her niece. "Well, since you refuse to help, I suppose I'll simply have to wait until the last minute, then call his hotel and leave a message that pressing business duties prevent me from dining with him."

That niggling little problem apparently taken care of for now, Marian's expression turned sympathetic. "So, how is he?"

"Mitch is fine, all things considered." Alanna wondered how many more times she'd have to repeat herself.

Marian waved away Alanna's answer with an impatient hand. "I know Mitch is fine. I saw him last night, reading that watered-down statement on the news. I was talking about Jonas."

"I don't know."

Marian arched a disbelieving silver brow. "You don't know? How could you not know how your own fiancé is holding up, during what has to be an incredibly stressful time?"

Alanna lowered her eyes to her lap, studiously avoiding her aunt's sharp gaze. "We haven't spoken since I sent him home from Washington to take his things out of the house," she admitted.

"What? Why on earth would you have him do that?"

Now it was Alanna's turn to pace. "Because it would have been too hard to explain to Mitch what another man's clothing was doing in my closet."

"Mitch is staying with you? At your house?"

"Where would you have him stay? On the street?"

"Why, I just assumed he'd be with Elizabeth."

"Elizabeth felt it would be better if Mitch went home with me."

"Of course she did. As his mother, she's required to act in his best interest. But what about your best interests? And Jonas's?"

"I'm going to work everything out," Alanna insisted.

Marian gave her a long, hard look. "I sincerely hope so, dear."

9

LATER THAT AFTERNOON, Alanna sat alone in her office, thinking back on that day she'd realized she'd fallen in love with Jonas. It was three months into the renovation, and they'd been painting the bathroom adjoining her bedroom. It had been his idea to do those rooms first, so she would have a sanctuary where she could sleep in a bed not surrounded by sawhorses and plaster dust.

"I thought you told me you were an expert painter," Jonas had said.

Alanna was on her knees, trimming around the edge of the bathtub. "I am."

"So how come you've got paint on your nose?"

She rubbed her nose with the back of her hand, spreading even more paint. "I said I was good. I didn't say I was neat."

"I suppose this is the price I have to pay for taking on amateur help." Jonas grinned down at her.

Rising to her feet, Alanna gave him a long, judicial look. "You've got paint on your face too, Mr. Professional," she pointed out.

"Where?"

"Right here." Taking her brush, she painted a long white swipe down the side of his face. "And here." Another across his forehead. "And here." His chin.

Jonas ran his wet brush down the front of her scarlet Save the Whales T-shirt. "At least I don't have it all over my clothes."

"Want to bet?" Alanna challenged, retaliating in kind.

Ignoring the fresh paint she'd streaked across his denim shirt, Jonas similarly marked her shorts and legs.

"Now look what you've done," she complained laughingly. "I'm a mess."

"You're right. We'd better clean you up before that paint dries." He turned on the shower and lifted her into the tub.

"Jonas—"

Before she could complain any further, Alanna found herself caught in a deep, wet, devastating kiss. She'd known the kiss was coming; she'd been expecting it for days. Weeks. There had been too many times when they'd be working together and their eyes would meet and hold for just a heartbeat too long.

Trembling, she reached for his hair. Her lips softened, yielded. "I've thought about this," she admitted breathlessly, when they came up for air. "I've dreamed about it. Wicked, wonderful dreams."

"Well?" His hand tangled gently, but possessively in her hair. "Does the reality live up to the fantasy?"

"I think so. But we'd better try again. Just to make sure." With her hands on either side of his head, she drew his lips back to hers. Her mind fogged, the world slipped out of focus. Feelings she thought she'd put away forever stirred again. She was alive. Alive!

A second thought followed quickly on the heels of the first. Mitch wasn't.

Jonas had sensed the difference in her immediately. "It's okay," he soothed, his large hand stroking her wet hair.

"You're going to hate me."

"Never."

His eyes, when she garnered the nerve to look up at him, were gentle and kind. "I can't do this." She drew in a deep, shuddering breath. "I wanted to.... Really.... But I can't."

His hands moved down her back, where they rested lightly at the base of her spine, as if to reassure her that he'd release her at the slightest protest. "I realize that it's difficult for you," he said solemnly. "But you don't have to do it alone, Alanna. I'll help you."

This time, when his lips touched hers, they remained light. Unthreatening. Now Alanna marveled at the way Jonas had obviously blocked out his own needs and concentrated solely on hers. When his lips had moved to her ear, she'd sighed. When they'd lingered at her neck, she'd felt a slow, kindling longing building again inside her. When he'd slipped his tongue between her parted lips, ripples of pleasure had washed over her.

Her head had spun as he undressed her. Hot steam swirled around them, warm water slid silkily off her pliant body, soapy hands caressed, aroused. Just when she'd thought her bones were going to dissolve, he'd lifted her from the velvet cling of water, wrapped her in a thick fluffy towel and carried her the few feet to her bed.

She'd been relieved when Jonas finally took off his own wet clothing. She wanted to touch him. To run her hands over his broad back, down his arms, across his chest. His body was hard and firm. Needing him to be strong, Alanna had reveled in his strength. But he had proved that he could be tender, as well. Tender enough for her to give herself to him without fear. Or regret.

His hands had remained slow, gentle. His clever lips coaxed and beguiled. Her mind clouded, so that when he finally slipped into her, Alanna wasn't certain if Jonas had actually told her that he loved her, or if the words had been born in her own imagination, of her own fevered wishes.

The insistent buzz of her intercom shattered the sensual reverie. "Yes, Karin?" she asked in a shaky voice, aware that it was nothing like her own usual controlled tone.

There was a moment's hesitation on the other end of the line. "Alanna? Are you all right?"

Alanna took a deep breath. "Fine," she said. "What's up?"

Before Karin could answer, the door to her office opened and Jonas entered. "She just wanted to warn you that your fiancé's here."

"Jonas. This is a surprise. Didn't you get my message?"

"I got it. But I decided to ignore it."

Although she had tried telling herself that it was anger over what he'd done to her beautiful bedroom, Alanna was forced to admit, if only to herself, that cowardice had made her unwilling to talk with him. She began unnecessarily tidying a neat stack of papers on her desk.

"Well, I'm sorry, but you're wasting your time because I have an extremely busy schedule and—"

"Why didn't you tell me you were going to sell the house?" He was towering over her, both hands pressed against the polished surface of her desk.

Thunderstruck, Alanna pushed herself out of her chair. "Where on earth did you get that idea?"

"From your husband. Your former husband," he amended, stressing Mitch's legal and, Jonas hoped, emotional status.

"You saw Mitch? You talked with him?" Dear Lord, she reflected wildly, what had Jonas done?

"Don't worry. I didn't let him in on our little secret. I was working on the library when he came downstairs. We exchanged a few words. He said something about what a good job I'd been doing and how it was too bad you weren't going to be able to see the house finished." He spoke with quiet deliberation, struggling to hold his temper in check.

Two thoughts were whirling around in her head. Jonas and Mitch had actually met. And Mitch believed she was still that adoring young girl who'd follow him anywhere at the drop of a hat.

"He's wrong."

"Is he?" His tone was deceptively mild, but for just a fleeting second, Alanna thought she saw a flash of vulnerability in his eyes, along with the banked anger.

"Absolutely." She pressed her palm against his cheek, feeling a muscle contract beneath her fingertips. Jonas had always been so easygoing; she couldn't remember ever seeing him so tense. "I love that house, Jonas. And I love you."

Jonas slowly released the breath he'd been unaware of holding. "Now that's the best news I've heard all day." He ran his hand down her hair. "How about having a long, romantic lunch on my boat? You can feed me grapes, and I'll let you drink champagne from my sneaker."

"Oh, Jonas . . ."

Jonas felt a new wave of fury and controlled it. "Okay, champagne and grapes are out. What would you say to dim sum at Tung Fong?"

"I really don't have time for lunch."

"Is it lunch you don't have time for?" Jonas asked. His fingers curved around her wrist. "Or me?"

He was all quiet intensity, understated strength. For too many months she'd been guilty of misreading Jonas, of only seeing the calm exterior, missing the passion that lurked just beneath the surface.

"You know better than that. Besides," Alanna shot back, aware that the stress of the past week was making her rash, "you have a lot of nerve behaving like the injured party here, Jonas Harte. After what you did to my bedroom!"

"Our bedroom." His fingers tightened, biting into her skin as jealousy clawed at his gut. "Or has your former husband's return made you forget all we've shared there? Perhaps I was just a substitute, something to ease the itch when the nights finally got too lonely."

Alanna recoiled as if he'd slapped her. "That's disgusting." She shook off his touch.

"Perhaps. But you can't blame me for thinking the worst when the woman I love refuses to talk to me, and the man she was once married to is making plans to sell her house and take her away."

"I'm not going anywhere," Alanna insisted.

"Try telling that to him."

"I will."

"When?" Jonas demanded.

Flinging up her arms, Alanna whirled away from him, retreating behind her desk. "Soon." She quickly discovered that the three feet of polished mahogany between them proved an ineffectual barrier.

"Dammit, that's not the answer I wanted," Jonas said. "But I suppose it's the one I'm going to have to accept for now." He went around the desk, reducing the gap between them. "But don't take too long, Alanna. Because I'm discovering that I'm not a patient man."

Before Alanna could respond, he closed his mouth over hers. The kiss was long and rough and strangely desperate. It also had the effect of a spark on dry tinder. Alanna felt reality slipping away from her. With a quiet moan, she wrapped her arms around him, her own lips greedy.

"I've missed this," Jonas said against her hair, after he'd finally broken away. "I've missed you."

"I've missed you, too," she whispered into the hard line of his shoulder. Lifting her head, she blinked away the tears stinging behind her lids. "I promise, everything will be all right. *We'll* be all right."

He wanted to believe her. But as he lowered his head for just one more kiss, Jonas couldn't quite shake the feeling that Mitchell Cantrell was in the room with them.

ANOTHER WEEK PASSED. A week that became increasingly difficult with each passing day. Although Jonas was no longer sleeping under her roof, it seemed to Alanna that he had claimed some sort of squatter's rights to her house.

He was already on the job, hammering away, when she came downstairs for her morning coffee. He was still there, hanging Sheetrock, planing doors, painting window trim, when she arrived home in the evening. If she thought the weekend might bring relief, she was mistaken. Jonas arrived, bright and early Saturday morning, professing an urgent need to sand the library floor. Sunday afternoon, when the incessant noise of the power sander had scraped her nerves raw, she stomped into the room and heatedly accused him of emotional harassment.

"That's a crock," he said after turning off the sander. The sudden silence, after two days of almost nonstop screeching, seemed deafening. "You hired me to do a job, lady, and that's precisely what I'm doing."

"So can't you do the floors some other time?" she demanded, glaring up at him. "When I'm at work? In case you haven't noticed, this is the weekend, Jonas. I'd appreciate a little peace and quiet."

"If you and your husband want peace and quiet, perhaps you'd better check into the Mark Hopkins," he said. "Because I have work to do."

That said, he turned the sander back on, forestalling Alanna's furious reply.

TWO DAYS LATER they were together again. Jonas had located a pair of windows in a Sausalito antique shop, windows he felt would be perfect for the library, and wanted Alanna to see them for herself.

"What do you think?" Jonas asked. They were standing on the sidewalk, looking in at the stained glass panes displayed in the wide front window of the shop.

"They're more than perfect," Alanna breathed. "They're exquisite."

The artist had created a stained glass landscape reminiscent of Tiffany's famed *Oyster Bay*. But in this case, the serene harbor in question was obviously San Francisco Bay. The warm sun slanting through the store window had turned the grapes that framed the water a deep, ripe purple, making them appear real enough to pluck from the vines. In the distance, the unmistakable orange towers of the Golden Gate Bridge gleamed copper in an iridescent sky.

"I thought you'd like them," Jonas said.

"I love them." When she took his hand, the tension that had been lingering between them dissolved. "You know," she murmured, "I've never seen them before, yet they seem oddly familiar." Comprehension dawned. "It's the view from my bedroom window!"

She was so clearly delighted with his find that Jonas allowed himself to relax for the first time in nearly two weeks. "That's what I thought. Look closer at the one on the left."

Alanna leaned forward to study the window in question. "Oh, my goodness, it's the whales!" Her fingers tightened on his. "Our whales."

So she hadn't forgotten. That, at least, was something, Jonas decided.

It was all Alanna could do to keep her enthusiasm in check, while she browsed through the cluttered hillside shop.

"This is nice." She ran her fingers lovingly over the graceful figure of a woman decorating a frosted perfume bottle.

She'd no sooner spoken when a clerk appeared from behind a towering suit of armor. "That just came in," he said. "It is, of course, an excellent example of Art Nouveau."

"Yes, it is." Alanna imagined how nice the bottle would look on her dresser. Once Jonas returned her bedroom to its former cozy state.

"Besides being beautiful, it's also functional," the clerk hastened to point out. "This ground glass stopper makes the bottle airtight."

Alanna glanced at the inflated price on the tag and sighed before turning away. "It is lovely, but I'm afraid it's a bit out of my range." For the next few minutes she continued to stroll idly through the cluttered aisles.

The clerk dogged her heels, stopping to point out a pressed glass peacock plate, a white bisque stoneware English mistletoe teapot, a Delft crocus pot.

"Everything is lovely," Alanna said, pausing in front of a red Chippendale chair, "but I'm afraid you don't have quite what I'm looking for."

The clerk's face revealed his worry that he was about to lose a customer. "Perhaps, if Madame could tell me what she's seeking . . ."

"The problem is that I don't really know," Alanna told him. She gave him an apologetic smile. "I'm afraid it's one of those cases where I'll know it when I see it."

For the next ten minutes the clerk remained undaunted, bringing various items to her attention: a beveled mirror with Japanese lacquer frame; an excellent copy of the bronze Medici Horse; a delicate silver picture frame, its design adapted from a seventeenth-century lace design. Each time Alanna shook her head and sighed.

"My wife is rather selective," Jonas explained to the frustrated clerk.

After an additional ten minutes, during which time the harried man grew increasingly desperate, they turned to leave. Just as they reached the door, Jonas spoke to Alanna.

"Those are rather nice." Both she and the clerk followed his gaze to the stained glass windows.

"They are," Alanna agreed noncommittally. "But I'm sure they must be dreadfully expensive."

"I suppose so," Jonas agreed. "And it's not as if those ones we looked at in Cow Hollow wouldn't do just as well."

It was a routine they'd perfected over the weeks and months of antique hunting. And it was definitely working today.

"I believe those particular windows were scheduled to go on sale today," the anxious clerk quickly informed them. "Let me check with the owner."

Five minutes later they were driving back to San Francisco, Alanna's purchases safely packed in thick layers of bubble wrap in the back of Jonas's van.

"I can't believe we actually got him down to that price!" Alanna beamed her delight. "When you asked him to throw in the perfume bottle, I was sure you'd blown the entire deal. But he agreed!"

Jonas shrugged. "He wanted to make a sale." He took her hand and laced their fingers together. "Besides, the poor guy didn't stand a chance. You and I make one helluva team."

When she viewed the uncensored love in his eyes, regret washed over Alanna for the untenable situation she'd forced Jonas into. A situation that had gone on for far too long.

"Yes," she said softly. "We do." She took a deep breath. "I'm going to tell him, Jonas. Tonight."

He lifted her hand to his lips. "And then you'll come to me."

She was doing the right thing, Alanna assured herself. It was time. It was past time. "Yes."

THAT AFTERNOON, when Alanna had returned to work and Jonas was out picking up the tile he'd need for the next day, Mitch took advantage of their absence and roamed the house, studying the books of wallpaper samples, fingering the swatches of fabric. She'd taken on a herculean task, he realized, glancing through the blueprints Jonas had left in the library. Although he was no architect, Mitch was able to see that this was more than a simple remodeling job.

"She'd have been better off letting a wrecking ball demolish the damn thing and starting over from scratch," he decided, his eyes widening at the cost sheet he found beside the blueprints.

Although she had assured him that the salary she earned at the magazine was generous, she'd obviously had to tap into her trust fund. Personally, Mitch found such expenditure a waste of money. To him, a house had always been just some place to hang your hat before going on to the next story. The next adventure.

He remembered when Allie had felt the same way. For not the first time since he'd returned home, Mitch was flooded with a perverse sense of estrangement.

He thought back to how she'd eagerly followed him to Beirut after their hasty wedding, despite her obvious fear and dislike of his dangerous life-style. Apparently his kidnapping had knocked some of the wind out of her sails; this rambling, ramshackle old house obviously represented safety. Security. Boredom.

No problem, Mitch assured himself. He'd simply have to coax the spark back into his beautiful bride. Remind her that there was a big, wonderful exciting world out there. He picked up the telephone, pleased at the idea of taking his life back into his own hands.

Fifteen minutes later, all the plans had been made. Immensely satisfied, Mitch went upstairs to change into his new blue suit. Allie would be home soon and he wanted to be ready.

10

It WAS AS IF she'd stepped back in time.

Alanna returned home from work to find Mitch, looking as handsome as ever in a navy suit, white silk shirt and maroon tie. To all but the sharpest eye, it would have been impossible to see any lingering signs of ill effects from his prolonged captivity. He was standing straight and tall, looking every inch the network star. The vibrant life had returned to his gleaming blue eyes, and the smile he greeted her with was as intoxicating as ever.

"It's about time you got home," he said, taking her coat and hanging it on the rack in the entry. "I was about ready to send out the bloodhounds."

"I'm sorry. I got delayed at the last minute."

"Problems?"

"None that I can't handle." She gave him a long, careful study. "Shouldn't you be in bed?"

"Now there's an idea."

Alanna blushed at his intimate tone. "I meant—"

"I know what you meant. And for the record, I'm fine." Other than a slight lingering headache, he felt better than he had in days. Besides, playing the invalid had become damn boring.

Alanna took the tulip-shaped glass he handed her. Dutch courage, she mused, taking a sip of the sparkling gold wine. To help her get through the next few hours. The champagne was crisp and soft at the same time, bubbling against the back of her throat.

"This is wonderful." Knowing Mitch's extravagant ways, she couldn't help wondering what he'd paid for such an exquisite vintage.

"Only the best for my bride," Mitch affirmed happily. His eyes glowed with the lusty good humor that had always been her undoing, but just when Alanna thought he was going to kiss her, he put his hand upon her back and led her to the stairs. "If you'll be so good as to come upstairs with me, M'lady. I have drawn Madam's bawth," he said, slipping easily into a British accent that would have sounded at home on Fleet Street.

Soon after her marriage, Alanna had discovered that Mitch's talent for mimicry had earned him an exalted place among his peers. How many evenings had she spent sitting quietly while Mitch entertained the press corps in the dining room of Beirut's Commodore Hotel, conducting mock interviews with renowned heads of state? Too many, she reflected now, wishing that she and Mitch could have had more time to themselves during that all-important first year of marriage.

Still, he was brilliant. Enough for word of his biting imitation of Great Britain's prime minister to get back to the Iron Lady herself. To Alanna's amazement, instead of being disturbed, the prime minister had written Mitch a charming letter, inviting him to dinner the next time he was in London.

"You know, I think Dan Rather was right when he said you should have gone on the stage," Alanna said, more to herself than to Mitch.

Mitch stopped in his tracks and looked down at her, genuinely surprised by her murmured statement. "But my dear," he said, slipping easily into his Sir Laurence Olivier accent, "I have. This is a bold new age. And television news is the biggest stage in the world." Sir Laurence gave way to the gravelly tones of Walter Cronkite. "And that's the way it is."

It was like a fever with him. An addiction. His eyes blazed with a fervor that would normally be associated with making love. How naive she'd been, Allie mused, thinking back on how she'd once been satisfied—no, more than satisfied, she'd been happy—to settle for being Mitch's second love. Because his work—the news—had always come first. And probably always would.

Proceeding to the next scene of his little play, Mitch opened the bathroom door with a flourish. The room glowed with the flickering light of a dozen fragrant white candles. The copper tub was filled with frothy bubbles, an open champagne bottle rested in a silver bucket beside the tub. The steamy air was sweet with the scent of baskets of dark red American Beauty roses.

It was, Alanna decided, staring at a display that could have come straight from the pages of a romantic novel, pure Mitch. He'd always enjoyed grand gestures, like those fragrant tulips he'd given her on that long-ago anniversary in Beirut.

"You'll never change, will you?" she asked softly.

"Would you want me to?" he asked, genuinely curious as to why her eyes were both sad and fond as she turned and looked up at him.

Alanna contemplated the question for a long, silent moment. What if Mitch could change? What if he spent less time creating these larger-than-life gestures and simply became more considerate about the little things? What if he were willing to forego being the network's hotshot foreign correspondent and settle down in a rambling house, filled with laughing children who crayoned murals on the dining-room wallpaper and brought home stray kittens?

What if he became more like . . . more like Jonas? she asked herself, knowing that it would be easier to keep the sun from rising in the morning than to change this man with whom she'd shared the most exciting, frustrating, frightening year of her life.

"No," she said truthfully. "I wouldn't want you to change, Mitch."

He nodded, supremely satisfied. For just one moment, as he'd watched the myriad of emotions cross her face, Mitch had wondered if she'd found someone else. Some other man to share her life with. But that was impossible, he decided now. Because he and Allie belonged together. He'd known that from the moment he returned home for his father's funeral and saw her standing in his mother's kitchen, looking so solemn. So sweet.

He reached out a hand to touch her cheek. When she took a step backward, Mitch decided that the blatantly seductive scene he'd set accounted for her nerves. Reminding himself that they had all night, he smiled.

"As much as I'd love to share those bubbles with you, I have a few phone calls to return. I seem to be a hot property these days. What would you think about my writing a book?"

Pleased that he'd ask her advice about such an important career opportunity, Alanna said, "I think it's a great idea."

Mitch grinned. "That's what I told my agent when he called this morning."

Alanna's own smile faded when she realized that he'd already made his decision. So why had he bothered to ask?

Mitch saw the flash of disappointment in her eyes and wondered what the hell he'd done wrong now. "Why don't you take your bath?" he suggested, hoping that after they'd made love tonight, all the tensions would fade and he'd realize he'd only imagined the enormous chasm that seemed to have opened up between them. "Our dinner reservations aren't until eight."

"Dinner reservations?"

"I've been kind of a dud so far, what with getting sick and nearly passing out in the Rose Garden and all," Mitch explained. "So I thought I'd make it up to you and save you the trouble of cooking."

"But—" Alanna decided that nothing would be settled by arguing. Perhaps it was better this way. Perhaps if they could just discuss the future in a neutral setting. "Where are we going?"

He bent his head and pressed a quick, hard kiss against her lips. "It's a surprise."

She tasted so sweet. So sexy. His body ached with the memory of her soft, feminine curves. Knowing that if he stayed another minute he'd drag her into that enormous copper bathtub and take her now, he backed away from temptation.

He bent down, broke off a velvety scarlet rosebud and slipped it into her hair. "Enjoy your bath," he said in a voice husky with desire—and left while he still could.

Alanna stood by the bathtub, fingers pressed against her lips, silent tears streaming down her cheeks.

MITCH HAD NOT BEEN foolish enough to expect things—people—not to change during his absence. But he had believed that every life had certain constants. One was that Alanna, as a native San Franciscan, would always share his liking for John's Grill, the restaurant where Sam Spade had downed an order of chops, a baked potato and sliced tomatoes in *The Maltese Falcon*.

He'd brought her here on their first date, pointing out the memorabilia and old photos on the wood-paneled walls. The place was a bastion of a romantic, bygone era, and if the prices had risen during his absence, Mitch wasn't about to complain. "So what did you expect, pal?" Spade would have inquired succinctly. "Nostalgia's always gonna cost you more."

The first time they'd come here, Alanna had waxed enthusiastic. Tonight, however, Mitch detected a distinct chill in the air.

"Something wrong?" he asked finally. "You've been pushing that prime rib around on your plate all night."

Alanna looked up. "I'm sure it's excellent. It's just that I don't eat red meat any longer."

She saw him stare at her as if she'd just grown an extra head. "Since when?"

"I don't remember exactly. It was kind of a gradual thing. Three, maybe four years."

"You're kidding."

"No."

Okay, Mitch told himself. So she'd joined the grain and granola crowd. He could handle that. "Why didn't you tell me?"

"You didn't give me a chance. You'd already given our order to the waiter before I could open my mouth."

If he didn't know better, Mitch would have thought Alanna resented him ordering for her. But that was ridiculous. He'd always done that. "I'm sorry. I thought it might be fun to relive our first date."

"It was a nice thought," she agreed, reaching out to cover his hand with hers. "But you can't relive the past, Mitch."

Her eyes were warm, but her hand was cold. "You can sure as hell try." Taking her hand between both of his, he tried rubbing some warmth into it. "Let's go home, sweetheart."

Alanna would have had to have been blind not to miss the banked passion in his eyes. "Mitch . . ."

"I've tried to be patient, Allie." He managed to keep his voice low. It wouldn't do for the network's returning star reporter to be seen yelling at his wife in public. "But I don't know how much longer I can wait to make love to my wife."

Tugging free of his light hold, Alanna closed her eyes for a moment, gathering strength for what she had to say. "That's just it."

Her face was as pale as a New England sky in February, her eyes were large and filled with pain. Mitch had the sudden feeling that he was standing on the edge of a precipice; the slightest push would send him falling to his death. Only years of public speaking under inordinate stress allowed him to keep his voice calm. "What's 'it'?"

"I'm not your wife."

"What?"

Before she could respond, the formally dressed waiter appeared beside the table to clear away. "Is anything wrong with your meal, ma'am?" he asked, looking pointedly at Alanna's untouched plate.

"No." She tried a smile that failed. "I guess I'm just not very hungry tonight."

"Perhaps you'd like to order something else. We received some fresh lobster this morning. If you'd like . . ."

"No." Alanna shook her head. "Thank you, but I'm really not at all hungry."

The waiter was nothing if not persistent. "Perhaps some dessert?"

"The lady said she wasn't hungry," Mitch growled uncharacteristically. "So if you wouldn't mind just bringing us the check—"

"Of course, Mr. Cantrell," the waiter said. "I'll be right back."

"Mitch . . ." Alanna began, once they were alone again.

"No." Mitch's intense blue eyes met hers. "Not here. Not now."

Biting her lip, she lowered her head and remained silent. After what seemed an eternity, the waiter returned with the manager of the restaurant. "Mr. Cantrell," the manager said, "it's a pleasure to have you back home."

Mitch forced the public smile he was a long way from feeling. "It's good to be back."

The manager's eyes slid to Alanna, who was struggling to maintain her composure. "I heard that you didn't eat a bite of your dinner, Mrs. Cantrell. Are you certain we can't get you something else? For Mitch Cantrell's lovely wife, the chef will be willing to fix anything you request."

"My wife isn't hungry," Mitch repeated yet again. "I think the excitement of having me home again has killed her appetite."

The manager seemed to accept the polite lie. "No doubt." When Mitch pulled out his credit card, he waved it away. "Oh, no, Mr. Cantrell," he insisted, "the dinner is on the house."

Mitch was in no mood to hang around and argue. "Thanks," he said. "And please tell the chef that the prime rib was delicious. As always."

Rising from the table, he took hold of Alanna's arm. "Come along, dear. I think it's time we returned home."

Accustomed to Mitch's temper, Allie found his icy silence on the drive home from the restaurant unnerving.

What only Mitch knew was that his unwillingness to talk was born of fear, not anger. Allie had dropped one helluva bombshell on him. He needed time to sort out his response, so he wouldn't blow what could well turn out to be the most important conversation of his life.

After they returned home, by unspoken, mutual agreement, both went into the kitchen. Not only was the homey room one of the few that wasn't in a shambles, it seemed to be the most neutral territory. "Would you like a drink?"

"I'm not supposed to drink while I'm taking this medication," he reminded her, matching her own polite tone. They could have been strangers, Mitch considered sadly.

"That's right. I'm sorry, I forgot."

"Obviously you've had a lot on your mind. I will take some coffee, though. If it's not too much trouble."

"Oh, no trouble at all." She was more than eager to do something, anything, to forestall the moment of truth. "Oh, damn," she said after lifting the lid of the copper cannister. "I used the last of the coffee this morning. I was planning to pick up some on my way home, but today was so hectic, what with all the messages piling up on my desk, and that damn Ramsey Tremayne's possible takeover bid, and—"

"Allie. Calm down," Mitch interrupted her nervous spiel. "Instant's fine."

Tension and distress filled her eyes as she turned toward him. "I really am sorry, Mitch."

"About the coffee? Believe me, sweetheart, I've had a lot worse."

That was exactly what was bothering her, what was making her feel so guilty. While she had been blissfully falling in love with Jonas, Mitch had been going through hell. When her eyes misted yet again, it crossed Alanna's mind that she'd probably cried more in the past few days than she had the past five years.

"I'm usually annoyingly efficient," she complained. "I can't figure out how I could have forgotten it."

"Perhaps you've had more important things on your mind," Mitch said mildly.

"Bull's-eye. Give that man a Kewpie doll." Turning away, she spooned a teaspoonful of instant coffee into a cup and put the kettle on to boil.

"It's my journalistic instincts," he said with a wry smile. "I'm famous for them."

"I know," Alanna said, relaxing somewhat as the conversation momentarily detoured to safer, more familiar territory. "When you nearly got yourself killed, covering that coup attempt in Latin America, *Time* called you the most brilliant man on television."

"That was *Newsweek*. *Time* merely said that I had a genius for discovering the single nugget of truth, hidden under a mountain of political manure."

"That same article also said that you brought an unparalleled depth to electronic journalism. That your coverage was both slick and intelligent at the same time."

"You actually remember all that?"

"Of course. I still have the clipping."

She would, too, Mitch knew. He'd been amazed when, after making love to Alanna for the first time, she had shyly shown him the scrapbook she'd kept over the years, filled with clippings of his exploits. He'd also been surprised, but inordinately pleased, to learn that she'd harbored a secret crush for him since her high school years.

"I've changed my mind," he said, going over to take the kettle off the burner. "I think I'd rather skip the coffee and just talk instead."

Alanna sank onto one of the chairs. "There's something you have to understand," she said, forcing herself to meet his eyes. "I didn't divorce you."

"Well, that's a good start." He pulled out a chair and sat facing her, knees nearly touching. "So if you didn't divorce me, and I sure as hell didn't divorce you, why aren't you my wife any longer?"

"I gave you the press clippings. Have you read them all?"

"Of course."

"Then you know that the State Department declared you dead three years ago."

"Sure. After the Islamic jihad claimed that they had executed me for high crimes against Islam. Actually, if you want to know the truth, I didn't think anyone would have believed that cock-and-bull story." This time his smile reminded Alanna more of the devil-may-care Mitch she'd fallen in love with. "I guess my own feeling of immortality is so deeply ingrained that I couldn't imagine the government, let alone my loved ones, thinking I could actually die."

"But we did," Alanna insisted shakily. She took a long, ragged breath, determined to get through this without crying. "I mean, the photograph was blurry, but all the government experts studied it for weeks and weeks, before finally declaring that the body was yours." A sob took up residence in her throat, shutting off her words. Alanna swallowed.

"We didn't want to believe you were dead. But the government was so sure. And there didn't seem to be any reason for your captors to lie. I mean, if their main purpose in taking you hostage in the first place was to use you for a bargaining chip, what sense did it make to announce your death?"

How must it have been for her? Mitch wondered. All alone, awaiting word of her husband's fate, only to learn that she was a widow before she'd had sufficient time to be a wife.

"Unfortunately, a lot of people in that part of the world don't seem to worry about things making sense." He frowned as he thought back to the insanity of the past five years.

Unable to bear the remembered pain in his eyes, Alanna lowered her head. "Oh, Mitch," she whispered.

Returning to the present, he took hold of her hand, linking their fingers. Her wedding ring gleamed in the muted light. "Hey. I sure as hell don't want your pity, Allie. Just your love."

Alanna looked down at their joined hands, recalling that blissful day when he'd slipped the gold band onto her finger. *Till death do you part*, the minister had said, leaving Alanna to believe that she and Mitch would have a lifetime together. Unfortunately, the minister hadn't mentioned anything about "holy war" radicals.

She knew he was waiting for an answer. But what could she say? Because as he toyed absently with her wedding band, she admitted that despite her love for Jonas, she still had deep feelings for Mitch. Feelings that wouldn't go away.

Mitch reminded himself that as horrendous as all this had been for him, it certainly hadn't been a cakewalk for Allie, either. And although he was growing more impatient by the moment, he reluctantly admitted that she might need more time to adjust to his seeming return from the grave.

"All my life I've lived by a damn-the-torpedoes, full-steam-ahead philosophy." He ran his knuckles down the side of her face. "It's not going to be easy, living in the same house and not making love to you, but I'm willing to try to be patient. For your sake."

She was a coward. There were no two ways about it. Even as Alanna told herself that she was merely stalling until Mitch got his life in order, until he was able to get back to work, she knew that she should tell him the truth—the whole truth—now.

"I can't promise that things will be the same," she hedged. If she couldn't be honest, the least she could do was not give him any false hope.

He winked. "Perhaps not, but I'm counting on my irresistible charm to win you over. After all, how many men get a second chance to court their wife in style? Although I hate admitting to any flaws, I'm afraid I have to plead guilty to rushing things the first time," he said. "This time we'll take things nice and slow."

"I've changed, Mitch," Alanna warned. "I'm not that impressionable young woman you swept off her feet."

"I know." He lifted her hand and kissed the tender skin at the center of her palm. "You've matured into an exciting beautiful woman, Allie. Believe me, I'm looking forward to the challenge."

Shaken by the bold, masculine promise in his blue eyes, she stepped away. "Mitch, it really is late. And I have a conference call with one of our free-lance writers at seven-thirty tomorrow morning."

He arched a brow. "Isn't that a little early? Even for a hotshot editor?"

Once again Alanna opted to ignore his not so veiled sarcasm about her work. She knew from past conversations that Mitch considered anything less than hard news merely "puff pieces."

"Not when the writer lives in New York and there's a three-hour time difference."

"Touché. Of all people, I should understand about working around time zones." Unwilling to banish himself to that lonely bed without touching her one more time, he let his hand linger once again on her cheek. "Sweet dreams, Allie, my love."

Knowing how Judas must have felt, Alanna closed her eyes against his gentle caress. "Good night, Mitch."

JONAS KNEW WHO IT WAS the moment the phone rang. When Alanna hadn't shown up by nine o'clock, he realized that once again, she'd been unable to tell Mitch the truth. He'd been sitting out on the deck of his boat, watching the soft, misty blur of lights that was the San Francisco skyline across the Golden Gate.

"Hello."

His gruff tone was less than encouraging. "I'm sorry it's so late," Alanna said, "but we were out."

"Out? To Elizabeth's?"

"No." Alanna paused. "Mitch was feeling better, so we went out to dinner."

"Sounds cozy."

"It was his idea. After I discovered that he'd made all these elaborate plans, I couldn't exactly tell him no, could I?"

"You certainly don't seem to be able to refuse the guy anything," Jonas shot back, his patience hanging by a single thread.

There was another, longer pause. "You don't have to snap at me, Jonas. . . . I told him."

Jonas sat up a little straighter. This was a surprise. "About us?"

"Not quite."

He should have figured as much. "Then what? That you weren't going to sell the house?"

"That didn't come up."

"It didn't come up?" Jonas repeated disbelievingly. "The man returns home and blithely decides to get rid of what you once alleged to be your dream house, and you don't think it's important enough to mention?"

"I'd planned to discuss it with him, but after I told him that I was no longer his wife, the conversation got sidetracked."

Well that, at least, was something, Jonas decided. At least, perhaps now, she'd take off that damn wedding ring. "I'm glad you finally told him. It was past time, Alanna."

"I know."

She certainly sounded down. And no wonder, Jonas considered sympathetically. It had to have been a brutal conversation; he only wished he could have been there to help her get through it.

"Look," he said, "it's late and you're obviously upset, with good reason. Instead of you driving to Sausalito, why don't I come into the city?"

"You can't," she said quickly. Too quickly, Jonas thought.

"Why not?"

"Because Mitch is still here."

"What?"

"You're the one who pointed out that it was late," she reminded him. "I couldn't exactly throw him out on the street at this time of night, now, could I?"

Much as he hated to admit it, she had a point. Still, it wasn't as if Mitch was destined to join the ranks of the city's homeless. "I'm sure Elizabeth would have been happy to take her son in."

"You don't understand."

"Believe me, Alanna, I'm trying."

"Mitch's entire world has been turned upside down. I think it's important that he have some stability in his life, at least until he's back on his feet."

"That stability meaning you."

"He needs me, Jonas." Her voice was so quiet that Jonas had difficulty hearing it.

So do I, he could have answered. "What he needs is to get back to his own life," Jonas countered. "Don't you think you're only hurting him worse by holding out all this false hope?"

"I've already explained that I'm no longer his wife."

"So you've said. But what you haven't told me is what he plans to do about that little legal snafu."

This time Alanna's silence was deafening. Jonas decided that you didn't have to be a rocket scientist to figure out Mitch Cantrell's next move. He was going to try and win his woman back. It was, Jonas thought grimly, the same thing he'd do, if he were in the newsman's place.

"That's what I figured," he said finally. "Look, Alanna, I've got an early flight tomorrow morning, so I'd better hit the sack. I'll call you in a couple days."

Alanna's heart lurched. "You're leaving town?"

It took an effort, but he refrained from asking if she really cared. "I told you I had that house to look at up in Washington," he reminded her. "The renovation on Orcas Island."

Of course. She remembered now. He'd told her about it last month. In another lifetime. She also recalled that since accepting the renovation would have meant being away for weeks at a time, Jonas had decided against taking the job. But that had been before Mitch's return. And before Alanna had put their marriage plans on hold.

"Yours isn't my only job," he said now, his voice falling to the lower registers, calling up a sexual tug deep inside her. "It's just the only one I take personally."

He wasn't giving up on her. Not yet. Relieved, Alanna hugged the phone closer to her ear, as if she could lessen the distance between them. "I really do love you, Jonas," she whispered.

"I know. Go to sleep, sweetheart. I'll call you from Washington."

"I'll be waiting."

After he'd hung up, Jonas was struck with a sudden urge to drive into the city, drag Alanna out of her beloved house, take her back to the boat and sail away to somewhere the press and her former husband would never find them. Tahiti, perhaps, where they could spend long, lazy days basking in the sun and drinking rum punches, and moonlit nights walking along the sparkling sands. He'd build them a cozy little grass shack beside a blue lagoon and, when they weren't feeding one another passion fruit, they'd make love. And babies.

The only problem with that romantic little scenario was that this very minute, sleeping under Alanna's roof was another man who had his own plan for her life. His own fantasies.

And although Jonas had never been afraid of competition, unfortunately, Mitch Cantrell appeared to have the inside track.

11

IT WAS ten minutes after seven the following morning when Alanna walked into her office to find Marian waiting for her.

"I didn't expect to find anyone here," she greeted her aunt.

"I knew you had that early call, and I wanted to talk with you before anyone else got in," Marian explained. "I tried calling you last night. You weren't home."

"Mitch and I went out for dinner." Ignoring her aunt's accusing tone, Alanna took the lid off the styrene cup of coffee she'd purchased from the vending machine in the hall.

"The answering machine wasn't on."

"Mitch has been getting so many calls from people wanting to cash in on his story, we decided to unplug the damn thing."

"Sounds as if he's coming out of this smelling like a rose."

Alanna took a sip of the too hot coffee. "Hardly."

"Alanna, dear, you know that I've never been one to interfere in your personal life, but—"

"I know what I'm doing, Marian."

"Do you?" Marian's narrowed eyes were shrewd. "I wonder," she murmured. Then, shaking her head, she said, "But, believe it or not, I'm really not here to discuss your love life."

Or lack of it, Alanna mentally added. "Then what's up?" An unpalatable thought occurred to her. "Don't tell me that Ramsey Tremayne has made an offer for the magazine?"

"No." Marian waved away Alanna's concern. "He doesn't even get into the city until this afternoon. It took a little digging, but I found out that he's got a meeting with the mayor at five, so I thought I'd wait until then to call his hotel and leave the message canceling our dinner engagement."

It wasn't like Marian to employ such subterfuges, Alanna considered. On the contrary, she'd never met such a direct person. There was something her aunt wasn't telling her. Something about Ramsey Tremayne. "If it isn't the Australian raider, then what's wrong?"

"Brenda called yesterday. After you'd gone home."

Alanna smiled, remembering that afternoon six weeks ago when the editor in chief had stopped by the office with her infant girl. At the time, Alanna had been struck by a surge of maternal instinct so powerful, it had left her shaken. "I suppose she's eager to get back to work."

"On the contrary." Not bothering to conceal her irritation, Marian reached into her alligator purse and extracted a cigarette from a silver mesh case. Lighting the cigarette with a slim gold lighter, she eyed Alanna through a thin haze of blue smoke. "She began the rather lengthy conversation by insisting that she couldn't locate a suitable nanny."

"I've heard it's extremely difficult."

"So Brenda says. But I wasn't buying her plethora of excuses for a minute. Eventually she broke down and admitted the truth. That she can't bear to leave the child in order to return to work."

Alanna repressed a smile as she took another sip of coffee. Marian was making it sound as though Brenda was committing a cardinal sin. Personally, Alanna couldn't think of anything more enjoyable than staying home with a baby as sweet as Brenda's Sara. She envied her.

"Well, that does change things, doesn't it?" she mused. "I suppose you'll be taking on her duties."

"No." The short answer came out on a stream of smoke. "You will be."

Alanna slowly put down the cup. "You have to be joking."

"You know I never joke about business, Alanna."

"But I don't know anything about being editor in chief."

"Nonsense. You've been doing Brenda's work for the past three months."

"But that was on a temporary basis," Alanna argued. "And whenever I had a problem, I could call Brenda."

"Not that you'll need to, but you still can," Marian told her. "We worked out an arrangement that allows her to do some free-lance editing and writing at home. Until she gets this fool motherhood thing out of her system."

How simple it must be for her aunt, Alanna mused. Always knowing what path was right for her. Never allowing herself to get sidetracked by those ordinary, day-to-day personal problems that plague mere mortals. Even Marian's multiple marriages and divorces hadn't slowed her down. She was truly the most focused person Alanna had ever known.

There had once been a time when Alanna had envied such single-mindedness. Indeed, when she'd first accepted the position on the magazine, she'd hoped to be just like her aunt. But then, three months later, Jonas had come into her life—and taught her that personal distractions could indeed be rewarding.

Alanna toyed with the silver ballpoint pen on her desk. "This isn't a very good time for me to take on any more responsibility, Marian."

"Nonsense." The older woman stood up. "You simply have to prioritize, Alanna, dear." She glanced up at the clock. "It's time for your call. We'll talk later." Refusing to listen to another negative word, she walked out of the office.

What had she gotten herself into now? Alanna wondered.

The rest of the day passed in a blur. The staff, although edgy from the rumors of a takeover, seemed to take Alanna's promotion in stride. And although she knew her aunt was playing dirty by leaking the news before Alanna could officially turn it down, she had to admit that she found the challenge exciting.

"It's only too bad your father's family dinner is tonight," Marian said, dropping by Alanna's office once again at the end of the day. "You and Jonas should be out celebrating."

"Jonas is out of town," Alanna said, taking a stack of yellow files from her cabinet. She had several hours of work left to do before the staff meeting tomorrow morning.

"Oh?" Marian's arched brow invited elaboration.

"He's giving an estimate on a house in Washington. He should be back in two or three days."

"Washington, D.C.? Or the state?"

"The state. The house is on an island in Puget Sound."

"Wouldn't that involve him being away a great deal?"

She felt her blood go a little cold at the reminder. "I suppose it would." What if the woman on Orcas Island found Jonas as attractive as she had? Alanna wondered. And what if, tired of the tension between them, Jonas succumbed to this unknown woman's charms? What if they had an affair? What if he decided to stay up there, instead of returning home to San Francisco? To her?

"Oh well," Marian decided pragmatically, "it's probably just as well."

"What does that mean?" Alanna snapped.

Marian looked at her curiously. "I simply meant that with the upcoming Thanksgiving issue, you'll have your hands full. It's just as well that Jonas has something to keep him busy."

As long as it isn't *someone*, Alanna told herself, experiencing a hot surge of something that felt uncomfortably like jealousy. "I suppose you're right," she said. "Will I see you at dinner?"

"Of course." For a moment Marian looked inclined to say something else, but then, apparently deciding against it, glanced at her watch. "I'd better go call the hotel and leave a message for that scoundrel, Ramsey Tremayne."

Her voice was tinged with an uncharacteristic nervousness, but engrossed in her own worries about what Jonas might be doing on Orcas Island, Alanna didn't remark on it.

THE SAN JUAN ISLANDS were scattered in the waters of Puget Sound like emeralds waiting to be strung together. Standing by the rail of the ferry boat, Jonas watched a flurry of gulls following a fishing boat chugging toward Bellingham. Their raucous, staccato cries echoed on the early-morning air. He took a deep breath, drank in the brisk scent of salt water and tried to reflect on the mystical beauty of the landscape. But when he viewed a pod of killer whales—the whales that had given Orcas Island its name—his mind flashed back to that suspended moment in Alanna's bedroom when he'd known they would be lovers.

The green and white ferry docked. Disembarking with the rest of the passengers, Jonas reminded himself that he'd come here to work. Unfortunately, he didn't know quite how he was going to concentrate on business when his mind couldn't stop thinking of Alanna.

THE MOOD DURING DINNER was decidedly strained. It was as if everyone had chosen sides. David, his allegiance to Jonas obvious, remained frustratingly remote. Alanna's father, however, was treating Mitch like a long-lost son, which Alanna found ironic, since he'd been a vocal opponent of the marriage. As the meal dragged on, Alanna was grateful that Marian hadn't shown up. Her aunt had never been one to keep her thoughts to herself.

Fortunately, the conversation remained fairly neutral until Alanna announced her promotion. Then the evening really began its downhill slide.

"Hey, congratulations," David said. His broad grin almost made up for his earlier distant attitude. "So how does it feel to be at the top of the masthead?"

"I don't know," Alanna answered honestly. "Things were too hectic to think about it."

"You didn't tell me you'd gotten a promotion," Mitch said.

Alanna took a sip of coffee. "There wasn't time," she pointed out. "I barely had a chance to jump in and out of the shower and throw on my clothes before we had to leave."

"Perhaps if you hadn't gotten home two hours late, you might have had more time to fill your husband in on what's happening in your life," he suggested quietly.

Too quietly, Alanna decided. From the moment she'd walked in the door this evening, she'd sensed the irritation surrounding him like an icy cloud. An irritation that was beginning to get on her nerves. After all those times he'd just taken off on a story with nothing but a quickly scrawled note, leaving her to wait and worry, how dare he criticize her for working late?

An uneasy silence settled over the table. Putting her spoon down, Alanna met Mitch's censorious eyes. "I tried to call," she said. "But the phone was busy."

"I was talking with my agent."

"Oh?" Alanna's father, Franklin Fairfield, forged his way into the conversation. "Good news, I hope?"

"Better than good," Mitch said. "The book offers are growing by leaps and bounds. It seems there are a lot of people out there in the publishing world who think I have a chance of pulling off a Pulitzer."

"I'd like having a Pulitzer prize journalist in the family," Franklin declared, conveniently forgetting Alanna's award for photojournalism. "I've always said you had it in you, haven't I, Alanna?" he asked, turning toward his daughter.

It took Alanna a moment to answer. How could he think she had forgotten his outburst of temper when he'd learned that she and Mitch had eloped? At the time he'd been so busy calling his new son-in-law an unstable influence in her life, the subject of a Pulitzer hadn't come up.

"Whatever you say, Dad," she murmured, exchanging a quick glance with David, who'd witnessed their father's fireworks that long-ago day.

"So," Franklin said, returning his attention to Mitch, "what house are you and your agent leaning toward?"

Alanna was not surprised when Mitch mentioned one of the top publishing companies in New York. His next words, however, were a surprise. "My agent set up a meeting with the publisher for next Monday."

"You didn't tell me you were going to New York," Alanna said.

Mitch gave her a long look. "As you so succinctly pointed out, we didn't have any time to talk after you came rushing in the door."

"How long will you have to be gone?"

"The business end of things shouldn't take more than a day or two. I'll want to drop in on the network offices, of course, have lunch with my agent and the publisher, then, if everything goes according to plan, you and I should be able to celebrate with a night on the town. Then I figured we could stay a few more days, see some shows, you could get in some shopping—"

"Mitch," Alanna interrupted gently, "aren't you forgetting something?"

He frowned. "No. I don't think so."

"My work," she pointed out. "I can't just drop everything and run off to New York."

"Alanna," Mitch countered, "this is important to me."

"But my work is important to me, too," she insisted. "Especially now. With my promotion, I have more responsibilities."

Mitch remembered a time when her husband was Alanna's chief responsibility. If there was one woman he never would have predicted to fall prey to the perils of feminism, it was his sweet, agreeable Allie.

"Why don't we talk about this when we get home?" he suggested on a low, warning note.

Frustrated at the way he was treating her, Alanna bit back a tart response and merely nodded her agreement.

"Alanna." Her father's deep voice shattered the tense silence. "Could I see you alone in the library for a moment?"

Alanna exchanged another brief look with David. This time his expression was openly sympathetic. "Really, Dad—"

"It'll only take a moment." He looked at Mitch. "You don't mind, do you, son?"

Although the younger man had always sensed his father-in-law's disapproval, tonight something had decidedly changed. Perhaps he liked having a hero for a son-in-law. Maybe, by overcoming the odds, Mitch had finally won Alanna's father's respect. Or perhaps it was something else altogether. Whatever. Mitch figured that at this point, he'd take all the help he could get.

"Not at all," he said easily. "It'll give David a chance to fill me in on the Giants' chances for a pennant this season."

Alanna held her tongue until her father had closed the library door. Then she turned on him, her words revealing her frustration with the situation. "I don't understand you," she said. "You never wanted me to marry Mitch in the first place. So why are you now treating him like your long-lost son?"

"I was against the match," he agreed. "But not because I didn't admire Mitch. I simply thought that his vagabond life-style did not allow for a wife and family."

"And now you've changed your mind?"

"Not really. But the marriage was your choice, Alanna. And now that your husband's returned, you belong with him."

"In case you've forgotten," Alanna pointed out, "Mitch is no longer my husband."

"A mere legal technicality. One that can easily be remedied," her father returned brusquely.

"And if I don't want to remedy it?" she asked softly.

He scowled. "You're still determined to marry that dropout."

"Jonas is not a dropout."

"Isn't he? What else would you call a man who'd turn his back on a successful career, in order to move onto a boat and begin working with his hands, restoring rundown, old houses?"

"I'd call him," Alanna said firmly, "the man I love."

The senior Fairfield shook his head in mute frustration. "I don't understand you anymore, Alanna. You used to be such an agreeable young girl."

Loving him in spite of his disapproval, Alanna put her hand on his arm. "That's just the point, Dad," she said. "I used to be a girl. But I'm a woman now. And I have to be allowed to make my own choices."

"If you've made your choice," her father said, with the incisiveness that had made him one of the country's top litigators, "then why is Jonas alone in Washington, while Mitchell is living in your house?"

Good question, Alanna admitted. And one she wasn't about to tackle right now. "Everything will work out," she insisted, wishing she could believe that. "You'll see."

Mellowing, Franklin gave her a brief, fatherly hug. "I hope so, Alanna," he said. "For your sake."

THE PHONE WAS RINGING when Alanna and Mitch walked in the door. Thinking it might be Jonas, she raced to answer it.

"Hello?"

Hearing the blatant hope in her voice, Mitch, on his way to the kitchen, paused in the doorway.

"Oh. Hello Jim. Just a minute." She covered the mouth-piece with her hand. "It's Jim Delaney," she told Mitch. "Remember, I told you he was senior editor."

How could he forget a guy who'd called at least a dozen times, the first day he and Allie had gotten back from Washington? "I'll make some tea."

Alanna flashed him a grateful smile. "This will only take a minute," she promised.

Five minutes later she was still on the phone, listening to Jim Delaney with one ear and the sound of pots and pans banging with the other.

"We'll just have to get someone else," she told Jim. "I know it's late. We'll all have to put in more overtime." She listened to the litany of complaints on the other end of the line. "I'll call the other editors tonight, we'll make lists of possible replacements and meet first thing tomorrow to brainstorm. All right?"

Her problem solved as well as it could be for the time being, she said firmly, "Good night, Jim. I'll see you in my office, eight o'clock sharp."

She hung up, debated making her calls immediately, then decided it would be better to break the news to Mitch first.

"I can't go to New York with you," she said when she entered the kitchen.

He was standing by the counter, his back to her, dipping a tea bag into a china cup. "Of course you can. You'll just have to juggle your schedule a little."

"It's not that easy."

"It could be. If you wanted it to be."

"Mitch—"

He turned around. "This is important to me, Allie."

"I know. But the magazine is important, too. And something's come up."

"And what catastrophe are you facing this time?" He didn't bother to conceal his scorn for what he considered her petty problems. "Did some advertiser cancel a lipstick ad? Did your restaurant reviewer drop dead from ptomaine? Or perhaps the model for your focus on lingerie showed up for her shoot eight months pregnant?"

Alanna glanced at the clock on the wall. She didn't have either the time or the energy for an argument. "You don't have to be sarcastic, Mitch. For your information, the writer assigned a major article in the Thanksgiving edition called and said that he's off to do a piece on the lifestyles of Tibetan monks."

Mitch stared at her. "You're refusing to go to New York with me because some hack writer wants to write a puff piece on a bunch of monks?"

Alanna stiffened her back. "What makes you think he's a hack writer?"

Mitch's temper was up and running. "He writes for your rag, doesn't he?"

"I can't believe you said that!"

Neither could he. Although he admittedly didn't like the way the demands of Alanna's job had interfered with their time together, he couldn't deny that her beloved magazine managed to be both intelligent and entertaining. "Look," he said, taking another tack, "I still don't see what some guy backing out of his agreement to write a Thanksgiving article has to do with us."

"It's not just an article," Alanna insisted. "It's the annual ski spectacular."

"So get another writer."

"That's what I'm going to do. But I don't have much time."

Mitch shot her an unbelieving look. "Allie, unless things have changed drastically during my imprisonment, Thanksgiving is in November."

"I know that."

"And this is July."

"I know that, too."

"So, what's the problem?"

"The problem is that we work on a five-month lead time," she said. "And right now, we're working on the Thanksgiving issue."

"That's the most ridiculous thing I've ever heard of. Any good writer worth his salt can crank out a respectable piece in a matter of minutes. Hours, at the most. Can you imagine what would happen if people had to wait six months to get their nightly news?"

"*San Francisco Trends* is not the nightly news."

Mitch folded his arms across his chest. "My point exactly."

So they were back to calling it a rag again. Alanna ground her teeth as they stared at one another across an ever widening gulf. "I have phone calls to make," she said finally.

"Fine," Mitch retorted. "And I'm going to bed."

"Fine." Alanna walked out of the room. Two minutes later, she heard the bedroom door slam. Inhaling a deep breath, she picked up the telephone receiver and began to make her calls.

ALTHOUGH SHE FELT like a wrung-out dishrag, by ten-thirty the following morning Alanna had everything under control. She'd located another writer who proved eager for a chance to visit and report on ski resorts in Colorado, California and Utah, even if it was off-season. A fan of Hemingway, who had written his immortal *For Whom the Bell*

Tolls on the deck of a Sun Valley ski lodge, the writer had suggested that he add Idaho to his itinerary. In no position to argue, Alanna had readily agreed.

She was just congratulating herself on a job well-done, when Marian strolled into her office, looking remarkably relaxed.

"We missed you last night," Alanna said, deciding not to comment on her aunt's uncharacteristic tardiness. Usually Marian was already on her third cup of coffee by the time the rest of the staff, Alanna included, arrived.

"I'm afraid I got held up."

"Oh? Did Ramsey Tremayne track you down, after all?"

"We ran into one another," Marian said offhandedly. "I hear you had a slight problem with the November issue."

"Nothing we couldn't handle," Alanna assured her. "So?"

"So what?"

"So is he or isn't he?"

"Is he or isn't he what, dear?"

Alanna couldn't believe her aunt's vague attitude. Only yesterday she'd been determined to fight Ramsey Tremayne's rumored takeover tooth and nail. This morning she was behaving as if her head were somewhere up in the clouds.

"Marian." Alanna eyed the older woman with growing concern. "Are you feeling all right this morning?"

"I've never felt better."

"So, is the rumor true?"

"What rumor, dear?"

"Is Ramsey Tremayne going to try to take over the magazine or not?"

"Oh, that." Marian reached into her purse and pulled out a gold compact. "No," she said, fluffing her blond hair with her fingers, "he's not."

"Then why did he want to take you to dinner?"

Appearing satisfied, Marian closed the compact with a decisive snap. "Really, Alanna," she said. "Why does any handsome, dynamic man take any single woman to dinner?"

"Are you saying—?"

"I'm sorry, dear," Marian said, "but I have an appointment for a facial at eleven. Then Ramsey and I are having lunch on his yacht."

"His yacht?"

"He just bought it yesterday. From some Greek shipping tycoon." She waggled her beringed fingers at Alanna. "I don't think I'll be back today, Alanna. But I know I'm leaving the magazine in capable hands."

With that she practically floated out of the office, leaving Alanna to stare after her in bewilderment.

THE DAY PASSED all too quickly, and Alanna was relieved when no additional problems reared their nasty little heads. As usual, she was the last to leave the office, but before turning off the lights she called Jonas, on the outside chance that he might have returned home early. When all she got was his answering machine, she decided against leaving a message. What could she say that they hadn't been over too many times already?

She had no sooner hung up than the phone rang. "*San Francisco Trends* magazine," she answered.

"Hi," Mitch said. "How's it going?"

She hoped he wasn't going to start in on her late hours again. She still hadn't fully recovered from last night's fight. "Not so bad."

"Did you find another writer for the ski report?"

"Yes. Not only that, we were lucky enough to find one who actually knows his way around a slope."

"That should help," Mitch commented.

"That's what I said." There was a slight pause; each seemed to be waiting the other out, Alanna reflected. "Did you call for some special reason, Mitch?"

"Actually, I did." He cleared his throat. "I've been thinking about last night."

Alanna sat down, leaned her head against the back of her chair and closed her eyes. "Me, too," she said softly.

"I hate it when we fight."

"Me, too."

"I especially hate it when I'm the one who's wrong."

Alanna's eyes flew open. She couldn't remember Mitch ever taking blame for their frequent battles. "Is this an apology?"

He chuckled. "I guess you could say it is. But if you quote me on that, I'll deny it to my dying day."

Alanna smiled. "Your secret's safe with me."

"Good." Alanna could hear the answering smile in Mitch's voice. "There was one other reason I called," he added.

"Oh?" Alanna couldn't hide the apprehension in her voice.

"Since we've had two less than successful dinners out in a row, I thought we might try and break the trend. Why don't I make reservations at a seafood house?" He hesitated. "You do still eat fish, don't you?"

"Yes. And dinner sounds lovely. May I suggest a place?"

"It's your city."

Although Mitch had been born on Russian Hill, Alanna doubted that he'd spent more than five days at a time in San Francisco since he'd gone off to college. In fact, before this little episode, the longest he'd ever remained in the city was the week he'd come home for his father's funeral. The week they'd fallen in love.

"I still have an errand to run," she told him. "Why don't I meet you in about half an hour at Scott's? On Lombard Street."

"I know it. Half an hour," Mitch agreed. "And Allie?"

"Yes?"

"I really am sorry."

Alanna sighed. "Me, too."

THE RESTAURANT, one of San Francisco's finest in a city renowned for its culinary achievements, provided an inviting atmosphere. The bar was oak-paneled, the tables were draped in white damask, the interior was softly lighted. And Mitch suspected the food was outstanding.

But he hardly tasted his fried calamari or fisherman's stew. Instead he watched Alanna's every move, feeling strangely disoriented, like a man in a *Twilight Zone* television episode, who'd woken up one morning and found himself living in a parallel universe.

If he'd needed additional proof that Alanna was not the same woman he'd married, watching her over dinner would have driven the point home, very firmly. It hadn't escaped his attention that she'd been greeted warmly by the entire staff, including the owner.

"I come here a great deal," she explained at his questioning look.

Mitch observed the confident manner with which she selected the wine, watched the ease with which she greeted various prominent table-hopping patrons and began to realize that the changes in Alanna were more than superficial. She was *not* the same woman he'd married. For the first time since his return, Mitch began to realize that he might lose her.

"When is Jonas due back?" he asked after they'd returned to the house, wanting to test her reaction to his unexpected question. He was beginning to fear he was putting the puzzle together.

They were standing outside Mitch's bedroom door. Alanna had come upstairs to bring him fresh towels. Now she stopped and looked at him, wondering what he was thinking of.

"Why?" she asked with a great deal more calm than she was feeling.

Mitch shrugged. "Just wondering. I was thinking that perhaps you should take him off the library and put him to work on the other bedroom. So you could stop sleeping on the couch."

His gaze was frustratingly shuttered. Deciding that she had only imagined the edge to his voice, Alanna said, "I don't mind sleeping downstairs."

"It can't be that comfortable," Mitch argued. "So when is he coming back to the city?"

"I don't know." Jonas had been due back yesterday, but whenever Alanna called, all she got was his answering machine.

Mitch would have had to have been deaf to miss the disappointment in her voice. "Well, I know it's none of my business, but I really think you ought to consider replacing him."

"Oh, I can't do that!"

Mitch noted the panic in her voice, but chose not to comment on it. "Why not?" he asked mildly.

"Well . . . because they're his plans."

"Which I'm sure he was well paid for."

"Yes, but dependable contractors are difficult to find, Mitch. And you said yourself that Jonas's work was remarkable."

"He's good," Mitch agreed grudgingly. "But he's still not the only guy in the city." Now that he'd found out what he wanted to know, Mitch decided not to push her into a corner. Especially not when he had to leave for New York tomorrow morning. "But it's your house," he said.

Alanna breathed a sigh of relief. The evening had gone so well; she hadn't wanted to find herself embroiled in yet another argument. She held out the towels. "Good night, Mitch."

"Good night, Allie. Alanna," he corrected. Somehow, his old name just didn't fit the sleek, competent woman she'd become. "Thanks for dinner."

She smiled. "It was nice, wasn't it?" Somehow they'd managed to make it from the appetizer through dessert without him saying a simple negative word about her work. Although that might have been because they'd spent the entire evening talking about his plans for the book.

He nodded. "Very." Something flashed in him. Something hot and quick, either jealousy or need. He started to go into the bedroom when, with a muttered curse, he turned back and yanked her against him. Ignoring her startled gasp, he kissed her.

His lips were hard, bold, aggressive, claiming hers with an intensity that took her breath away. She tensed, then tried to back away, but as his hands slid under her silk blouse to warmly roam her back, her body began to remember what her mind had forced it to forget.

His searing lips molded hers to the shape he preferred, his hands skimmed over her flesh, inciting thrill after thrill. Time melted away. Then something changed. While his kisses had once exhilarated her, now they frightened her.

"No." She turned her head. "I'm sorry, Mitch. I can't."

Drawing away, he took his time studying her. "Can't?" he asked. "Or won't?"

"Please, Mitch.... Don't push."

It was the vulnerability in her wide eyes that proved to be his undoing. "Hey, it's your call." He stepped back so they were no longer touching, then realized he wasn't quite ready to break contact. "You know," he said, running his thumb along her cheek in a warm, slow sweep, "all this enforced celibacy would be a lot easier if you'd gotten fat and ugly in the past five years."

Alanna managed a weak smile. "I'm sorry."

"Don't be. It wouldn't have really mattered, since you'll always be beautiful to me." He touched her hair. "I'm going to miss you."

Though her throat was dry, she managed to speak evenly. "You said it was only going to be a few days."

"I know. But after losing you for five long years, every minute we're apart seems like an eternity." His quiet declaration made Alanna feel as if a shard of glass had suddenly been embedded in her heart. "Are you sure you can't come to New York with me?" he asked suddenly.

"Oh, Mitch—"

"I know." He dropped his hand, slipping it into the pocket of his slacks. "I'm pushing again." When he smiled at her, a crooked boyish grin that she'd thought she'd never see again, he looked remarkably like his old self. The devil-may-care man she'd had a crush on for as long as she could remember. "Patience has never been my long suit."

This time Alanna knew her smile was less forced. "Try telling me something I don't know."

Memories swirled in the air between them. Warm, comfortable, happy memories. "It's late," he said finally. "And I've got an early flight tomorrow morning." He leaned forward and pressed his lips against hers. The kiss was quick, light and confident. "Good night, sweetheart. Sleep tight."

He was inside the bedroom before Alanna could answer. She stood statue-still, fingers against her tingling lips. "Good night, Mitch," she finally whispered to the closed door.

12

ALANNA WAS WORKING harder than she'd ever worked in her life. The job of editor in chief was every bit as demanding as she'd feared. And every bit as fulfilling. In a way she welcomed the long hours, the constant emergencies, the frantic activity that increased exponentially as the magazine's deadline approached. Because when all her attention was on her work, she couldn't think of Jonas. Or Mitch.

It was only late at night, when she'd left the office behind and was all alone in the dark, that the two men she'd loved would appear to her in a myriad of ways, like facets in a child's kaleidoscope. Her future was with Jonas. She knew that. Yet how could she stop remembering how Mitch had once been the most important person in her life? He'd been the sun, around which her entire world had revolved; feelings like that didn't just go away because she might want them to.

It was then, during those long, lonely hours, that she'd wonder what would have happened if those terrorists hadn't abducted Mitch. Would they still be wildly in love? Would the very sight of him walking in the door leave her breathless? Would she still be following him all over the world, biting back her growing frustration while waiting for him to settle down?

If she had thought she'd be able to sort out her confused feelings while both men were out of town, Alanna realized she'd been mistaken. Instead, her mind continued to turn the problem over and over, like a leaf caught in the swirling eddies of a whirlpool.

"You look terrible," Marian announced, the third day of Mitch's absence. Returning from a long weekend and announcing she had something to celebrate, Alanna's aunt was treating her to a lunch at the Four Seasons. And although it was the first time Alanna had eaten lunch away from her desk in two weeks, she discovered that she had no appetite for what she knew to be a superb crab salad.

"Thanks a lot," Alanna said dryly. "It's always nice to hear kind words from your loved ones."

"Speaking of loved ones," Marian slipped in smoothly, "have you heard from Jonas lately?"

Alanna unenthusiastically pushed her lettuce around on her plate. "If you don't mind, Marian, I'd rather not discuss my personal life."

She saw her aunt's shrewd eyes narrow, but Marian appeared willing to accept her niece's wishes. For now. "Then I suppose we have no choice but to talk about mine," she said.

Alanna put down her fork, her interest piqued. She knew that Ramsey Tremayne was still in town; pictures of Marian and him had appeared almost daily in the society pages. But Marian had remained steadfastly close-mouthed whenever Alanna broached the subject, saying only that the Australian publishing magnate had no interest in purchasing *San Francisco Trends*.

With all the instincts of a born actress, Marian stretched out the moment. Reaching into her alligator bag, she pulled out a pack of cigarettes and her gold lighter.

It was when she lighted the cigarette that Alanna noticed a canary diamond the size of Rhode Island gleaming from the ring finger of her aunt's left hand.

"Is that what I think it is?"

Marian held out her hand, clearly admiring the way the dazzling stone splintered the light from the chandelier overhead. "A wedding ring," she confirmed. Her voice was calm, controlled, as if she dropped such a bombshell every day. "And a rather nice one, if I do say so myself." Her self-satisfied smile reminded Alanna of a cat eyeing a bowl of fresh cream. "Probably the nicest I've ever received."

Thinking of the queen's ransom of jewels her aunt had collected during her previous marriages, Alanna decided that was really saying something.

"You got married? To Ramsey Tremayne? But I thought you hated him."

"I did," Marian said calmly. "But that turned out to be a bit of a misunderstanding on both our parts." She paused to take a sip of her chardonnay. "Ramsey and I go back quite a few years," she admitted. "We were correspondents for competing wire services when we met at a conference in Geneva. It was lust at first sight." A small, reminiscent smile tugged at the corners of her lips. "Over the years we fell into a series of brief, no-strings affairs whenever—and wherever—our paths would cross.

"But then, during an assignment in Egypt, right before the Six-Day-War, things began to get more serious. In fact, for a time I found myself considering marriage. The morning the war broke out, I was down at the corner market, getting us some fruit and coffee for breakfast. Unfortunately, Ramsey's local contact arrived at the hotel to tell him that Egypt had attacked, and when he found me gone, he mistakenly thought that I'd dashed off to the battle site in order to scoop him. Despite our affair, we'd both remained fiercely competitive."

"I see," Alanna said, trying to follow the story as best she could.

"Well, anyway, naturally when I arrived back with my figs and coffee and discovered that Ramsey had left, I thought the same thing." Marian smiled and shook her head. "Fortunately, Ramsey recently decided that the time had come to bury our respective hatchets, and well, one thing led to another, and before I knew it, I was standing in front of a justice of the peace in a Reno chapel."

"I'm pleased that you and Ramsey worked out your misunderstanding," Alanna told her aunt. "But I still can't believe you ran off and got married without a word to anyone in the family."

"Oh, pooh." Marian waved away Alanna's protest. "In the first place, I seem to remember you and Mitchell doing precisely the same thing. And in the second place, since none of you have been at any of my other weddings, I saw no reason why this one should be different."

"All the other times you were off in some faraway country, chasing down a story," Alanna pointed out. "The last I heard, there weren't any direct flights to the Khyber Pass."

Marian smiled reminiscently. "Dear Mustafa," she murmured. "He was the only man I married who didn't have a cent to his name. But what he lacked in afghani, he definitely made up for in . . ." Soft color drifted into her cheeks. "Well, anyway," she said briskly, "I knew that you had enough on your hands these days. And your father, my dear, staid brother, would simply have launched into one of his lengthy lectures about the sanctity of the marriage contract."

"I've heard that one," Alanna said. "Quite recently, as a matter of fact."

"I'm not surprised. My elder sibling is nothing if not predictable," Marian observed dryly. "Which is probably the reason I've always been the family rebel. By the time

I was born, the role of the responsible Fairfield child had already been taken." She covered Alanna's hand with her own, and her expression turned momentarily serious. "Don't let your father pressure you. No matter what he says, Mitch is the wrong man for you."

"You sound so sure of that."

"I am. Because your former husband and I just happen to be peas from the same pod, darling. He can no more settle down than I could, all those years when I was determined to become the next Margaret Bourke-White."

"But you have settled down," Alanna argued. "You moved back to San Francisco and started the magazine, and even married again." A thought suddenly occurred to her. "You are staying in the city, aren't you?"

"Of course. At least for now. Ramsey enjoys living here, and all his newly acquired American interests promise to keep him in the country for some time." She gave Alanna a long, warning look. "But the thing you're overlooking, Alanna, dear, is that it took me sixty-three years to even begin to consider putting down roots. Mitch is only thirty-nine. Do you really want to wait another twenty-four years for him to tire of living out of a single suitcase?"

Although it was exactly what she'd been telling herself for weeks, a deep-seated sense of loyalty had Alanna defending Mitch. "He's been through a lot. You don't know that he hasn't changed."

"Men like Mitchell Cantrell never change," Marian said knowingly. "I heard about your little tiff during your father's dinner party. You can't tell me that he hasn't already shown signs of resenting your work."

Alanna didn't bother to try to deny her aunt's accusation. "It's only because his own life is so unsettled," she insisted.

"It's because he's grown too accustomed to being the center of attention to ever allow you your own life," Marian countered. "While Jonas has always encouraged you to take new risks. New challenges." She returned her attention to her Cobb salad for a moment, before looking again at Alanna. "Jonas is the man you should marry."

"I haven't said I wasn't going to marry him," Alanna snapped, suddenly conscious that fatigue, stress and the tension of the past weeks had caused her temper to flare. She took a deep breath. "I'm sorry. It's just that all this has been so difficult."

"Of course it has," Marian agreed soothingly. "But as dark as things look now, all this will pass. Things always do. And there's one thing you should keep in mind in the meantime."

"What's that?" Alanna asked glumly.

"All men, no matter how special they seem at the time, can easily be replaced."

Point made, Marian signaled their waiter for the check.

MARIAN'S WORDS rang over and over in Alanna's head during a long, restless night. She still couldn't get them out of her mind the following morning, when she was seated at her desk, studying a glossy colored layout the art department had sent up, depicting the season's hottest ski wear. Despite her aunt's apparent willingness to cease her constant globe-trotting, the one thing that obviously hadn't changed was her casual attitude toward men. Her belief that they could be so easily replaced.

Although Alanna admired her successful aunt in many ways, she knew how fortunate she'd been to love—and be loved by—two such extraordinary men in one lifetime, knew that this was one case where Marian was wrong.

As if conjured up by some magic spell, the phone rang, and she heard Karin's disembodied voice over the intercom. "It's Jonas. On line two."

Alanna stared at the blinking orange light as if it were a cobra, poised to strike. Taking a deep breath that was meant to calm but didn't, she picked up the receiver.

"Hello?"

"Do you have any idea what day this is?" Jonas greeted her without preamble.

Alanna's eyes cut to her desk calendar, where the date was circled in red. How on earth could she have forgotten the day she was to have been married?

"Oh, Jonas," she said on a sigh, "I really have messed things up, haven't I?"

"That's what I'm calling about."

"Oh?" *Please*, she thought, gripping the receiver tightly, *don't tell me that you're calling the whole thing off!*

"David tells me that Mitch is in New York."

"Yes."

"He also tells me that you opted not to go along."

"I had work to do. Honestly, Jonas, it's been ridiculous. You can't believe all the emergencies that have come up, and—"

"Alanna," Jonas broke in, "slow down and tell me one thing."

"What?"

"Is work the only reason you didn't go?"

"No."

There was a moment's silence as the significance of that single word reverberated over the telephone line. When Jonas finally spoke again, Alanna noticed that his husky voice was not as controlled as usual. "Can I take that to mean you're free for dinner tonight?"

He hadn't given up on her, after all! "Oh, yes," she breathed.

"I'll pick you up at seven."

Seven. Eight long hours. She wasn't certain she could wait that long. "Make it six, and you've got yourself a date."

"Six it is," he said. "I thought we'd eat on my boat. If that's okay with you."

"I'd love it."

After she hung up, Alanna left her office, stopping by Karin's desk. "I'm going to be out the rest of the day," she said. "But if any emergencies come up, I'll be getting my hair done. The number's in my book."

"Hot date?" Karin asked, curiosity bright in her eyes.

Alanna felt herself smiling, really smiling, for the first time in weeks. "You might say that."

"It's about time," Karin said. "Oh," she called out, just before Alanna reached the elevators, "in case you're interested, they're having a sale at Victoria's Secrets."

It did not escape Alanna's notice that Karin's little news bulletin had caught the attention of everyone in the office. Even as the color rose into her cheeks, she decided that it certainly wouldn't hurt to pay a visit to San Francisco's famed lingerie boutique.

JONAS HATED the uncertainty he felt driving into the city. Accustomed to maintaining control over his life, he'd found the past three weeks both frustrating and frightening. Even tonight, when he should have been on his honeymoon with his new bride, he was afraid of what he'd find when he arrived at Alanna's house. She'd sounded eager to see him this morning, but he'd already discovered that her moods changed with quicksilver speed these days. With his luck, he'd show up at her door at the same time

Cantrell was arriving home from New York, he thought blackly.

But that didn't happen. When she opened the door, looking like a vision from a fairy tale in a floaty, off-the-shoulder, sea-green silk dress, her hair piled loosely atop her head, her grandmother's pearls gleaming in her ears, Jonas promptly forgot his earlier aggravation.

"You look lovely."

She'd lost weight; Jonas knew her body intimately and guessed the loss to be somewhere between five and ten pounds. Pounds she could ill afford to lose. But to him she could never be anything but beautiful. "That's new, isn't it?"

Alanna was relieved. Trying on dress after dress this afternoon, she'd been dismayed at how thin she'd become. But apparently the change in her figure had not been as bad as she'd feared. She smiled. "Brand-new. I bought it this afternoon and I'm glad you like it, since I ended up spending the upstairs carpeting budget."

Jonas's eyes widened. "The whole upstairs?" He'd known women who spent a king's ransom on clothing, but Alanna had never been one of them.

Her smile warmed, until he thought he could feel its heat infiltrating his blood. "It's a special night," she said simply, as if that explained everything.

It did. Or at least enough for now. "I've missed you," Jonas told her.

"Not as much as I've missed you," she said honestly. She glanced down at the flowers he was still holding in his hand. "Are those for me?"

He looked down at the red roses. "Oh dear. Did you want some, too?"

The little bubble of tension that had been hovering over them burst. Alanna laughed and flung her arms around his neck. "Oh, Jonas, I'm so very glad you're back."

As he drank in her scent, Jonas silently concurred. Tossing the roses onto the butler's table, he wrapped his arms around her and buried his lips in her hair. "Not as happy as I am to be back."

She tilted her head to one side; he brushed a finger down her cheek, following the slow, seductive movement with his eyes. When he gently traced the soft outline of her mouth, her lips parted expectantly. "I thought about you," he said, drinking in her flushed face, the desire—*dear God, please let it be love*—that shone in her eyes. "All the time I was gone, I kept thinking about the way you look, imagining it was your scent floating on the breeze, driving me to distraction."

His hand trailed down her throat. "At night I thought about the way you fit so perfectly in my arms, remembered the way your eyes widen when I'm inside you."

His deep voice was making her body soften, a slow, enervating passion was flowing through her veins. Their lips met and clung—then suddenly it was over, much too soon.

"I promised you dinner," he said in a deep, husky voice that was none too steady.

Alanna bit back her own disappointment. "We could stay here and send out for Chinese."

The offer was very, very tempting. It was the first time in three weeks that he'd felt a spark of the old Alanna. Jonas had the uneasy feeling that if they allowed this mood to slip away, they might not get it back. It would be so easy to stay here and share a Chinese dinner, feeding one another bites of cashew chicken with plastic chopsticks, sharing egg rolls and roast pork with plum sauce. They'd drink a little too much wine, they'd laugh, he'd tell her about Orcas Island, she'd tell him about the magazine, and then they'd make love. All night long.

The scenario was decidedly appealing. The only problem was that Jonas couldn't quite shake another image. That of Mitch returning home to find another man ravishing his wife. *Former wife, dammit*, he reminded himself.

He realized that Alanna was looking up at him, waiting for his answer. "I promised you a romantic dinner on the boat," he said finally. "I think we'd better stick with our original plans."

The mood had changed. Only slightly, but Alanna could feel a wall going up between them. The same wall that had seemed to grow higher and more forbidding with each passing day. "I've always enjoyed your boat," she murmured, trying to keep the disappointment from her voice.

The first thing Alanna noticed when she entered the cabin was her wedding dress hanging on a hook beside the door leading to the bedroom. "I never did thank you for taking it with you."

"I thought it might be best under the circumstances."

He saw her eyes, earlier laced with passion, turn grave. "Still, you could have saved yourself a lot of grief by precipitating things."

Jonas shrugged. "Forcing the issue your first night home would only have caused you pain. Which would have ended up hurting me even more than this damned separation."

Alanna began twisting her hands together. Jonas noticed that she was no longer wearing her wedding band, but couldn't really take that as a positive sign, since she wasn't wearing his ring, either.

"What would you say to calling a moratorium on this conversation until after dinner?" he asked.

Alanna's relief was patently obvious. "I'd say that's a wonderful idea."

Crossing the compact living space, she sat down at the table, draped unfamiliarly in white damask. A red rose lay beside her plate, reminding her that she'd forgotten to put Jonas's roses into water before leaving the house.

"I hope you're hungry," he said, lighting the two white candles in the center of the table.

"Starving." What with getting her hair done and shopping for the perfect dress, not to mention the lacy fantasies she was wearing underneath it, she hadn't had time for lunch.

"Good. I'll confess that I didn't spend the afternoon over a hot stove, cooking this myself," he said, leaving her to go into the galley. "But I think you'll enjoy it, just the same."

Alanna's eyes widened when she viewed the first course he set in front of her. A rich, lobster bisque, laced with the unmistakable scent of vanilla beans. It was what she'd planned for the first course of their wedding dinner.

"I thought it might be appropriate," Jonas answered at her questioning glance. "While we might have had to postpone the ceremony, I couldn't think of any reason not to enjoy a dinner that took you and the caterer a month to plan."

It was exactly the type of gesture that Mitch would have thought of. And totally unlike Jonas. Did he actually think he had to compete with her former husband? Alanna wondered. Her next thought was even more distressing. Perhaps he was right. Perhaps she had been comparing the two men unfairly.

"It's perfect." She lowered her gaze so he could not see the sudden moisture welling up in her eyes.

She certainly didn't seem pleased, Jonas reflected, wondering what the hell he'd done wrong now. He'd come up with the idea on the flight back from Seattle. Not accustomed to setting up artificially romantic scenarios, he'd tried his plan out on David who'd pronounced it a sure winner. "I'm glad."

They ate their soup in an increasingly uncomfortable silence. Finally Alanna decided it was time one of them said something. Anything.

"How was your trip?"

He shrugged. "Rainy. But I saw a lot of whales."

Her eyes brightened with interest. "I wish I'd been there."

"I wish you'd been there, too," he agreed. He glanced significantly at her bowl. "Are you finished?"

So much for small talk, Alanna told herself bleakly. "Yes. Thank you." She forced a smile. "It was delicious."

She'd barely touched it. So far his grand gesture was going down in flames. Frustrated, Jonas turned inward. "You're the one who selected it."

"Tell me about the house," she said, when it appeared their second course would be as silent as the first.

Jonas looked up from his salad—endive, watercress and butter lettuce, with warm goat cheese marinated in thyme and caper sauce. It was typically Californian and as delicious as Alanna remembered. Unfortunately, her appetite seemed to have disappeared.

"What house?"

"The house you went up to Orcas Island to look at."

"Oh, that house." He shook his head. "I decided against taking the job."

Relief was instantaneous. "Oh, really? Why?"

"Because I decided this was a lousy time to be away from the city." His eyes met hers and held. "Or perhaps I was wrong."

The question was in the air, hovering between them. "No," Alanna said quietly. "You weren't wrong, Jonas."

It didn't escape Jonas's attention that she wasn't exactly telling him that he was right, either. Damn, but it hurt to sit here across the table, feeling her withdrawing more and more with each passing second. How long could they go on like this? he wondered. How long could he go on?

"That, at least, is something," he muttered, pushing back from the table and taking their plates into the galley.

The entrée was a flaky, dark pink fillet of Alaskan salmon with sun-dried tomatoes, fresh basil and alfalfa sprouts. Two months ago, when the caterer had first prepared it for her, she'd professed it to be a bit of heaven. Tonight the salmon tasted like ashes in her mouth.

"What was she like?" Alanna asked.

"What was who like?"

"The woman who owned the house. Is she married? Does she have children?" *Did you find her irresistible?*

"Oh. Jill. She's divorced," Jonas divulged, wondering where this line of questioning was leading. "No kids. More wine?"

Jill. The woman now had a name. A simple, carefree name. It was the name of a woman who probably would never give a man any problems, Alanna decided. She was about to refuse Jonas's offer of more wine. Then, deciding that a bit more alcohol might calm her nerves, she said, "Thank you. I think I will."

He filled her glass to within a half inch of the brim. *Good move, Harte,* Jonas told himself with disgust. *Get the lady drunk. Candy's dandy, but liquor's quicker, right?*

Alanna knew that the image of a seductive, gay divorcée luring men into her bed, was one of society's most hurtful stereotypes. But that didn't stop her from wondering.

"How old is she?" Her fingers nervously stroked the stem of her glass. "What did she look like?"

Alanna's unconscious gesture was unnervingly erotic. Jonas wondered exactly how he was going to get through this dinner when what he wanted to do was to rip off that flirty little dress and taste her skin. Skin that he knew would be as soft as it was fragrant.

It took an effort, but he managed to force his attention back to their conversation. "Why?"

"I was just trying to get a mental picture of her. After all, we do have similar tastes in houses. I was wondering what else we had in common." *Like you, Jonas,* Alanna silently added. *Do we have you in common?*

"She was in her early forties, I suppose. Blonde. Slender, but not too skinny, if you know what I mean."

Unfortunately, Alanna knew all too well what he meant. Once again she compared herself with the absent Jill. Once again she finished in second place. "She sounds charming." She was unable to keep a slight edge from her voice. "No wonder it took you so many days to turn down the job."

Jonas studied her with renewed interest. Was that actually jealousy he heard in her voice? The thought was heartening. A jealous woman was not an indifferent one.

"I had to wait a couple of days for her to get back," he explained easily. "She'd been painting in the Olympic Forest, and a rainstorm had washed out the trail."

"She's an artist?" This was getting worse and worse. Jill was a stacked, blond, divorced artist, who could undoubtedly offer a man a myriad of sexual pleasures without any accompanying complications.

"Oils. Her work sells mainly in the Northwest, but she's beginning to garner wider spread interest. In fact, the reason she wasn't there when I arrived was that she was trying to meet her deadline for her first New York show."

"I'm so pleased for her," Alanna said dryly.

Unsurprisingly, the dessert turned out to be the chocolate quenelle with vanilla maple sauce she'd selected. Alanna breathed a sigh of relief when the wedding cake she'd also planned to serve did not appear.

Her wedding dress, along with the meal that had been planned to celebrate what should have been the happiest day of her life, had already forced her to face exactly what she had given up. If she'd been confronted with that towering, white confection, she probably would have burst into tears.

"This isn't working very well, is it?" Jonas asked later, as they sat beside one another on the sofa.

The fog was beginning to come in, but Alanna could still see the lights on the buoys that guided the boats safely out of the Bay. *There should be buoys in life*, she mused. *Showing the way*.

Under normal conditions Alanna found the gentle movement of the boat soothing, but there was nothing remotely normal about this evening. Only three short weeks ago, she'd been about to marry the man she loved. A man who loved her. Now a chasm as vast as the Grand Canyon had opened up between them, one she worried might be too wide to breach.

She frowned, unable to look at Jonas. "I'm sorry," she murmured, gazing down at her hands, twisted together in her lap. "It's all my fault."

Jonas sighed. "It's not anyone's fault," he said, unlinking her hands and lacing his fingers with hers. "It's just the situation. Every day it goes on we seem to lose a little bit of ourselves."

"Don't you think I know that?" Her eyes finally lifted to his. Distressed, they appeared even wider than usual in her thin face. "Don't you think I hate living like this?"

"Then do something about it."

He made it sound so simple. As if her feelings for Mitch were nothing more than a current she could switch off and on at his request. "It's not that easy," she insisted, tugging ineffectually on her hand.

His grip tightened. Her hand was trapped and so was she. "It could be," he insisted in a calm, quiet tone that was only dangerous because of the intensity she could sense beneath his words. "You know, I really couldn't stop thinking about you, all the time I was gone. To tell the truth, I don't have any idea what that damn house looked like, because all I could see was your face. Looking at me the way you did that day we were painting the bathroom, your beautiful, soft eyes brimming over with desire, silently begging me to make love to you, because you couldn't quite get up the nerve to ask me out loud. Because it had been too long since a man had looked at you in that way. Touched you. Made you cry out."

A warm flush darkened her cheeks. "Really, Jonas," she protested, hating the way her voice trembled, "I remember everything about that day. You don't have to—"

"Everything?" he broke in gruffly. "Then you must remember me telling you I loved you."

Dropping her eyes once more, she nodded. "At the time I wasn't sure whether you'd said the words, or whether I'd imagined them."

Her quiet admission was the opening he'd been waiting for. "You thought you might have imagined them, because you wanted me to say them."

"Yes," she whispered raggedly.

"Because you wanted me to love you."

"Yes, dammit!" she shouted, her nerves reaching their shattering point, like a crystal wineglass hit by a high note. "I desperately wanted you to love me, because I'd fallen in love with you. Is that what you wanted to hear, Jonas? Does that finally soothe your wounded male ego?"

Appearing unfazed by her show of temper, he drew her to him, holding her tighter when she resisted. "You got what you wanted, Alanna," he reminded her. "We both got what we wanted. I suppose one of our problems is that I probably should have warned you of something that day."

"What?" His face was suddenly so close. His eyes so dark.

"I've always believed that love was something deeper than wanting. More permanent than need. That's why I never—ever—told a woman I loved her until you."

She swallowed, her heart in her throat. "I do love you, Jonas."

He heard the hesitation in her soft voice. Fainter than before, but lingering there, just the same. "But?" he asked quietly.

Alanna took a deep, ragged breath, knowing that she owed Jonas the truth. "But I can't deny or forget that I loved Mitch, too." She looked up at him, her eyes glistening. "Perhaps it wasn't the mature love I feel for you, but it wasn't a teenage crush, either." A tear trailed down her cheek. She absently wiped it away with the back of her hand. "Well, perhaps it started out as a crush," she admitted, "but when I married him, I really, truly loved him."

Seeing her this miserable, on what should have been the happiest night of her life, did nothing to ease Jonas's own pain. But the situation had become untenable. He supposed he could live with her decision, if she chose Cantrell. His heart would probably feel like a stone—a deadweight inside him—but in a way, losing Alanna would undoubtedly be a great deal like losing his father to death. There would be an intense, seemingly overwhelming period of pain, followed by days, even weeks of grief, then months, perhaps even a few years of mourning. But he'd survive. As he always had. The thing he couldn't live with, what was tearing him in two, was the uncertainty.

"I stopped by Laura's house early this evening, before picking you up," he said. Laura, the eldest of his five younger sisters, was an eighth-grade history teacher and mother of five children, all under the age of ten.

Alanna looked at him curiously, wondering why he'd abruptly changed the subject. Not that she wasn't grateful for the sudden detour. "How is she?"

"Terrific, as usual. And harried. Having one kid go through the terrible twos is probably bad enough. She swears that twins are not merely twice the work of the other three at that age, but ten times."

"I can imagine," Alanna said softly, thinking how many times she'd envied Jonas's sister her happy brood.

"Roger was feeding the kids hot dogs for dinner," he continued in that same, seemingly casual tone that Alanna didn't quite trust. "Laura had locked herself in the bedroom and was grading papers. Watching her, something occurred to me."

Here it was, Alanna thought. Whatever it was Jonas had been leading up to. "What's that?"

Ignoring the decided lack of enthusiasm in her tone, he said, "I decided that life is kind of like a multiple choice test." His eyes, as they met hers and held, were unnervingly grave. "Two or three answers may seem to fit, but there's only one that's ultimately right."

Alanna got his point. Loud and clear. "You're telling me that I've run out of time," she said flatly.

"This has gone on long enough," he concurred. "If Cantrell is well enough to be running around New York, he sure as hell is well enough to learn the truth about me. About us."

"Jonas—"

"No." He put up a hand. "Let me finish. When all this started, I thought maybe the problem was that you didn't really want to make a decision. Cantrell and I are opposite sides of the coin. Perhaps you liked the idea of two different men to appeal to different sides of you. Then I began to think that I had it all wrong. Maybe this wasn't about different men, but about you being two different women. Maybe you liked flying high with him, while at the same time knowing that if you got too high, when the air got too thin and you were about to lose your bearings, you could always return safely to earth with me."

How could he think something so terrible about her? was Alanna's first thought. Her second, and the most unattractive one she'd had all evening, was that perhaps he was right.

"But the important thing," Jonas continued, "is that on the flight back from Seattle, it dawned on me that it didn't matter whether you loved two different men or wanted to be two different women. Because, although I've always considered myself a reasonable man, I can't—I won't—continue to share you."

He framed her face in his hands, his expression as pained as she'd ever seen it. Yet resolved, Alanna saw. "You have to make a decision, Alanna." His lips hovered over hers, tempting, threatening, she couldn't tell which. "Now."

"What do you want me to do?" she asked. "Call Mitch at the hotel and tell him that I'm sorry, but I'm with another man, the man I love? And although I'm sorry for all he's been through and I truly wish him the best, I'm asking him not to come back to San Francisco, because it might disrupt my perfect life?" she added pointedly.

Tears streamed down her face. "Why can't you understand?" she begged. "Right now, Mitch is all alone. I'm all he's got. I can't turn my back on him!" she cried out. "No matter how much I love you. And no matter how it's tearing my heart in two."

Jonas had grown up in a houseful of women; he was accustomed to their tears. He also knew that some women—perhaps most—could use such tears as a weapon. Or for defense. But Alanna's ragged sobs were being torn from her unwillingly, born of pure, heartrending grief. He was still frustrated. Still angry. But he knew that neither emotion would do anything to help them out of the morass they seemed to have stumbled into.

Jonas cursed softly. Then drew her into his arms. "It's going to be all right," he said, his lips against her hair. "Somehow we're going to get through this, Alanna. Together."

Drained, Alanna could not answer. Instead, emotionally exhausted, all she could do was cling to him.

The night grew dark. And still they sat there, Jonas's arms around her, Alanna's cheek pressed against his chest. There were no more tears in her, but the sorrow remained, like a cold stone inside her chest. Water lapped softly against the boat; in the distance she could hear the lonely sound of a foghorn.

Hours passed. Her thoughts drifted to Mitch—memories of how she'd worshiped him from afar during her impressionable teenage years, had fallen in love and agonized over his disappearance, of how she'd grieved his death. And then, and only then, how she'd chosen to go on with her life. She thought of Jonas—from the life they'd forged over these past months to the gleaming future they'd planned together.

From the slowness of her breathing she could have fallen asleep, but Jonas knew she was awake and thinking. Of whom? he couldn't help wondering. Himself? Cantrell? Both of them?

"Feeling better?" he asked quietly.

She sighed. Then nodded. "It's late," she said in a thin voice. "I'd better go home."

"You're welcome to stay here."

"I know." His face was shuttered, but she could see the ravages of pain and lingering passion in his dark eyes.

This time it was she who framed his face in her hands. "I do love you," she said, suddenly intense. And before he could answer, she'd crushed her mouth to his. "I'll always love you."

13

HER AVID LIPS, as they clung to his, said more than words. Her hands, as she struggled with the buttons of his shirt, before pressing herself against his chest, revealed a primal need as old as the sea. Desperate for more, she uttered a low, pleased sound in her throat and she placed the imprint of her open mouth upon his warm skin.

This was no prolonged seduction, followed by a lingering lovemaking. They were ravenous, feeding from each other as if it had been an eternity since they'd tasted this hot passion.

It was torture. He was throbbing so hard, he thought he'd explode. It was ecstasy. He pulled the silk dress from her in a frenzy, stopping only for a brief, aching moment to admire the picture she made, clad only in a white satin, lace-trimmed teddy, a pair of thigh-high ivory stockings and her cream silk pumps.

Kissing her deeply, he slipped his fingers under the high-cut leg of the teddy. Her breathing quickened, and her body quaked as his thumb stroked the sensitive bud. When he twisted his fingers together and slipped them into her, she cried out his name, but the sound was muffled by his mouth.

Alanna trembled as the world peeled away. Hunger made a mockery of control. Alanna couldn't question it. She couldn't refuse it. All she knew was that she'd never needed a man as she needed Jonas at this moment. Her excitement was almost unbearable. Fire and ice coursed through her. Her body was like a furnace, as heat from his lips seeped into her bloodstream; sharp, needlelike chills raced over her flesh. Wrapping her arms around him, she drew him closer, daring him to take more.

There was a sound of tearing silk. Then his hands were running bruisingly over her, kneading, possessing, creating flash points of pleasure that were just this side of pain. Jonas was lost in the feel of her. The taste. The scent. His mouth followed the path his roving hands blazed, teasing, taunting, taking her beyond sanity, beyond the civilized, to a place of speeding wind and black sky. Half-mad, her body was stunningly alive as they struggled against the remaining barrier of his clothing.

Her urgent need for him was unreasonable, but Alanna was beyond reason. Uttering greedy, desperate demands, she arched against him, twining her fingers into his hair as she drew his mouth back to hers. Their bodies were hot, slick and moist. Heart pounded against heart. Desire spun into delirium.

They came together savagely. Alanna's fingernails dug into his hips as he plunged into her with an intensity that made her cry out. Then she felt herself beginning to fill, fill to the desperate point of shattering. Unable to stop, he continued to drive them up and up to a crest that seemed unattainable, a place where the air was thin, and breathing almost impossible. Just when she thought she couldn't take any more, she felt herself suddenly flung off the edge of the world. Entire galaxies were exploding around her, whirling, blinding spheres of flame; even the long, spiraling fall back to earth was a shattering thrill.

She couldn't stop the shudders. Her bones were like water, and even if Jonas hadn't been lying on top of her, Alanna knew that she couldn't have moved if her life depended on it. It took a major effort even to lift her lids and meet his gaze.

His eyes were shuttered, like windows painted black. Nothing had changed, Alanna realized bleakly. Nothing at all.

But Jonas was looking down at the bruises that were beginning to darken her fair skin and cursing himself. Even at his most passionate, he'd never harmed a woman before. Until Alanna. The one woman he'd rather cut out his heart than hurt.

"I'm sorry," he said finally.

His remote tone caused her heart to lurch. "I wanted it as much as you," she reminded him quietly.

"I wasn't talking about that," he said. "I was talking about the way I was so rough." He drew his lips together into a tight line as he observed a dark purple shadow on her breast.

"I'm not porcelain, Jonas," she said. "I won't break.... I didn't want you to be gentle. In fact, if you want to know the truth, I think I needed you *not* to be." She ran her finger down the gouges on his back. "Besides, you won't be able to take your shirt off for at least a week."

Jonas sat up. In a bleak gesture she'd never seen before, he rubbed both hands over his face. "You'd better get dressed," he said. "I'll take you home."

She was inclined to argue, but changed her mind. Gathering up her dress and shoes—her teddy was ruined—she disappeared into the bathroom. *The head*, she reminded herself as she zipped up the back of her dress. Jonas was always teasing her that if she was going to be the wife of a weekend sailor, she was going to have to learn to call things by their nautical names.

They remained silent on the drive back to her house. The first word either spoke was when they were standing at her door; Jonas suddenly pressed some bills into her hand.

She looked down at them blankly. "What's this for?" Surely he didn't mean . . . ? No, he couldn't, she assured herself wildly.

"It's for that lacy thing I ripped."

"Oh. The teddy. You don't owe me anything, Jonas. If you want to know the truth, I rather enjoyed that part."

He smiled. For the first time since they'd left this house hours ago. "So did I. I'll buy you another."

"You?" The thought of Jonas actually walking into Victoria's Secrets and selecting a piece of replacement lingerie had Alanna smiling, as well. "Why do I see you sending one of your sisters on that little errand?"

It wasn't often Jonas blushed. This was one of the few times. And even as he damned the color he felt rising from his collar, he realized that if his embarrassment could ease the tension between them, so be it. "That just goes to show how little you know about me," he said. "I'll make you a deal. You and I will go together, and you can model everything in the store, so I can decide upon a suitable replacement."

"If tonight was any example, we'd probably end up getting arrested for indecent behavior before I managed to get into the second outfit."

This time his smile reached his eyes. Little lines fanned outward from the warm depths. He ran his palm over her tousled hair. "If tonight was any example, it'd probably be worth risking jail." He looked down at her and thought he'd never seen any woman as beautiful. Her lips were full from being thoroughly kissed, her hair was a chestnut tumble, her skin glowed. He wanted to take her upstairs and spend the rest of the night making slow, gentle love to her.

But he couldn't. Or at least he wouldn't. Not as long as the only bed upstairs belonged to Mitch Cantrell.

"I'd better get going," he said, his voice husky with renewed desire.

"Are you certain you can't come in for coffee?"

He shook his head. "I'd better not. It's late. And you've got work in the morning."

"What about you?" Now that he'd turned down that other job, wasn't he going to return to work on her house? Alanna didn't want to admit that what she really wanted was Jonas back under her roof. In her life. Where he belonged.

"I'm going to take the boat out for a couple days."

"Oh." She tried to keep the disappointment from her voice. She failed. "Will you call me when you get back?"

It was the hardest thing he'd ever done. "No. I don't think so."

"But what about my house? We have a contract." It wasn't the house. But pride was suddenly a small, fierce thing, and Alanna couldn't admit that she was terrified of losing him.

"I'll make sure the work gets done, Alanna. But I don't think it'd be a very good idea for me to do it."

"But I love you," she protested.

"And I love you." He traced the line of her trembling lips with his thumbnail. "But that doesn't always seem to be enough, does it?" he murmured. "Good night, Alanna."

He turned and walked down the steps. Alanna stood under her porch light and watched until the taillights of his car disappeared around the corner. Then she began to shiver.

Alanna entered the house, picking up the roses that had already begun to wilt. The little red light was blinking on the answering machine when she entered the kitchen.

Knowing instinctively who had called, she sighed and pushed the button.

"Hi, Allie!" Mitch's deep, unmistakable voice filled the room. "I guess you're working late. I tried the magazine, but there wasn't any answer. The switchboard must be down for the night. Anyway, I'm sorry I missed you, but I thought you might like to know that I'm coming home tomorrow with some dynamite news...." There was a pause, as if he were trying to decide exactly how much to tell her. "I'll fill you in on all the details when I get there, okay? Love ya, sweetheart. Sweet dreams."

If the tone of his voice was any indication, things had gone well in New York. Better than well. The only time she'd ever heard Mitch so excited had been when he'd scooped one of his competitors on a big story. He must have gotten a big advance for his book, she decided as she got ready for bed.

But as she lay alone on the lounge in the downstairs parlor, she could not help thinking that whatever had Mitch so excited was more than a book contract. He was going away again. She knew it. The problem was, she couldn't quite shake the feeling that he expected her to go with him. And why not? she asked herself honestly as the long, sleepless night dragged on. Hadn't she once gone traipsing off to Lebanon without a backward glance?

The problem was, she admitted now, she'd hated going. She'd hated leaving her family, her job, her friends, to go off to live in a war zone. And she'd hated being there. She'd hated the daily bombings, the killings of innocent children; every time Mitch disappeared, often for days at a time, she'd hated the way her stomach tied up in knots. In fact, the doctor at the American University Hospital had warned her that if she didn't learn to relax, she was going to end up with an ulcer before her twenty-fifth birthday.

Alanna had tried. She'd attempted self-hypnotism, biofeedback, visualization. When none of that worked, the doctor had prescribed exercise, but one time when she was riding her bike along the Rue Hamra, a bomb had exploded in front of the *An Nahar* newspaper offices, moments after she'd passed. So much for exercise.

Finally she'd tried to adjust by downplaying her own fear and concentrating on her husband's obvious zeal for his work. But even that had proved ineffective. Eventually, the only times that Alanna hadn't wished that she was back in the States were when Mitch made love to her. Unfortunately, they could not spend all their life in bed.

Unable to sleep, Alanna returned to the kitchen and put on a pot of coffee. She turned on the radio, twisting the dial until she found a classical station that was playing some Chopin, which should have been soothing, but wasn't. She changed to an all-night, talk radio station instead.

Later, as she sat in the dark, sipping her coffee and listening to all the other lonely people who were finding sleep an elusive target, Alanna wondered if this night would ever end.

THE FLIGHT out of La Guardia had been delayed forty-five minutes. Forty-five minutes that to Mitch seemed an eternity. He was anxious to get back to San Francisco. To break his news to Alanna, but most of all, to have that talk they'd been putting off for far too long.

Despite the fact that he was anxious to discuss the future, Mitch was not yet prepared to tell her about the past five years. Besides, he rationalized, Alanna probably wouldn't really want to hear the gritty truth. After all, ever since his return, it had been his experience that most individuals, while expressing grave regret for what had happened, were afraid to hear any of the details. It was preferable, safer even, to think of his ordeal in the abstract. An unpleasant facet of modern life that they might view on the evening news.

As the plane reached its cruising altitude of thirty thousand feet, Mitch thought about how much his life had changed since that day, six years ago, when he'd first made love to Allie. Sometimes that sunny, idyllic day seemed like yesterday; at other times it seemed that it had happened in another lifetime.

That they'd both changed was obvious. There was a distance between them that had not previously existed. But it was to be expected, he told himself. After all, their whirlwind courtship had not allowed them sufficient time to get to know one another. And as for their first year of marriage, even he had to admit that it was difficult to build lasting foundations in a place where daily shelling was destroying everything around you.

But that was his life. And he'd certainly never lied to her. Allie had known at the time what she was getting into.

But had she really? his inner voice questioned. Allie had been young and very, very naive; it had been easy to sweep her off her feet. She had clearly admired him; something close to hero worship had shone in her eyes, and if he was to be perfectly honest with himself, Mitch knew that he'd have to admit that he'd enjoyed her unqualified devotion.

That was then. And this was now. Allie was now a self-sufficient career woman who was obviously on a professional fast track. A woman who would not be so likely to welcome having her life turned upside down. Again.

He sighed. He and Alanna were definitely going to have to have a long talk about a great many things. Including Jonas Harte.

AT THE SAME TIME that Mitch was thinking about his rival, Jonas was sitting on the deck of his boat, drinking coffee with Alanna's brother. His red-veined, darkly shadowed eyes revealed his lack of sleep.

"Are you sure you know what you're doing?" David asked.

Jonas rubbed his unshaven cheek. "Hell, no. But after the way dinner went last night, I decided things sure couldn't get any worse."

"She could choose Mitch."

"She isn't going to do that."

"You're that sure of her?"

"No," Jonas said firmly. "I'm that sure of us." His jaw jutted out, his gaze remained steady. "The thing is," he said, "she has to realize that for herself. If I force her hand, there's an outside chance she'll spend the rest of her life wondering if she made the right decision. I have to trust in her instinct to do what's right. For her. And for both of us. And when she comes to me—and she will," he insisted gruffly, "I want it to be without reservations."

"And if she doesn't come to you?" David asked quietly.

"Then I'll just have to kidnap her, sail off into the sunset and keep her on this boat until she changes her mind."

Both men laughed, but the sound held little humor.

ALANNA WAS WAITING for Mitch when he walked in the door. He found her in the sun room. One look at her pale face, the shadows like bruises beneath her tired eyes, her trembling hands, told him all he wanted to know. Obviously, his wife did not find this homecoming to be a joyous occasion.

"Are you all right?"

She managed a smile. "I think I'm supposed to ask you that question."

He waved away her concern. "I'm fine. In fact, the network insisted I have another physical while I was in New York. The doctors said I was as healthy as a mule."

"I think it's as healthy as a horse and as stubborn as a mule."

His smile was quick and appealing. "They said that, too." Despite his attempt at levity, the tension lingered, hovering over them like an early-morning fog that had yet to burn off.

"I would have picked you up at the airport," Alanna said, "but you didn't tell me which flight you were taking, and when I finally thought of calling the hotel, you'd already checked out."

"That's okay. The network sprang for a limo."

Mitch sat down on the sofa beside her and put his arm around her. Although she stiffened ever so slightly, she did not turn away, something he took to be a good sign.

"It's time we talked," he said.

Alanna nodded, her heart in her throat. "Yes."

Unreasonably nervous himself, Mitch played with the ends of her hair. A sudden memory flashed through his mind. A memory of how that silky hair had felt, draped over his chest after making love. "The network gave me a new assignment."

"Oh?" Alanna looked at him curiously. "What about the book?"

A smile teased at the corners of his lips. "You know me, Allie. I could never spend a year or whatever it took, sitting at a typewriter."

The advocate in her, the woman who'd worked unceasingly for hostage rights, momentarily steamrollered over the wife who'd been sitting up all night trying to raise the nerve to tell her husband that she was in love with another man. "But it's a story that needs to be told," she insisted. "You weren't the only one, Mitch. There are other hostages who need your help. Our help."

He saw the fire in her eyes and recognized it immediately. It was the same passion he felt for his own work. It was also the same passion she used to reserve solely for him. "Don't worry, honey," he said. "I'm not going to dodge my responsibilities."

He took a deep breath, remembering the other hostages he'd met during his captivity. Men who'd helped keep him sane. "I'm not as self-centered as you must think. I understand that I owe something to the others. But I promise you, Allie, this new assignment isn't going to interfere with my writing the book."

"They offered you the anchor spot," she guessed.

"They did. And I turned it down."

Alanna wondered why she should be the slightest bit surprised. "Again."

"Again," he confirmed. "You know me, Allie, I'd go crazy in that job."

Yes, she agreed, he would. "Just like you'd go crazy staying in one place for very long," she murmured.

It was true. Part of him, the part that wanted a home and a wife and a family, wished it wasn't. But another, stronger part, always needed to see what was around the next bend. He knew Alanna was happy here, he could see that she'd put down some very substantial roots. But despite his desire to spend the rest of his days making love to her, the thought of passing his life in one place, even in a city as lovely as San Francisco, in a home as perfect as the one she was so lovingly restoring, made him feel something akin to claustrophobia.

He took another deep breath, then asked the question he'd been putting off for too long. "You're not going to come with me this time, are you, Allie?"

She'd known this was coming. But she hadn't expected it to be so painful. "No," she whispered, looking down at her hands. "I'm not."

He wasn't surprised. But that didn't stop her answer from hurting. "Is it Jonas?"

"Not really. Oh, of course Jonas is part of it, but..." His words sank in; Alanna looked up at him, surprised. "How did you know?"

Mitch shrugged. "Hey, I'm the hotshot reporter here, remember? It wasn't that difficult to see that my wife had fallen in love with another man."

"It wasn't like that," she heard herself protest shakily. "I thought you were dead, and I'd been alone for so many years, and then Jonas came along, and—"

"Alanna." Mitch pushed her hair back from her face and held her unhappy gaze to his. "You don't have to explain. You also have nothing to apologize for."

"I've felt so guilty."

Her wide eyes were misted and filled with pain. Even so, she was still the most beautiful woman he'd ever known. Mitch doubted that he'd ever meet anyone else who made him feel the way he did when he was with his Allie.

"Guilt is a self-defeating emotion. Besides, you have nothing to feel guilty about." His gruff voice was not as steady as he would have liked. "I only have one question."

"What?"

"Does he make you happy?"

"Yes." It was little more than a cracked whisper. She sniffled. "Yes," she repeated, a bit stronger.

His heart was breaking, but Mitch managed a smile, nonetheless. He found it ironic that years of hiding his emotions in front of the camera were proving a rehearsal for this, the most difficult conversation he'd ever had in his life.

"I'm glad." He tugged lightly on the ends of her hair. "I hope the guy realizes how lucky he is. I also hope that he knows that if he's not good to you, Allie, he'll have me to answer to."

And he would, she knew. The love she and Mitch had shared was not gone. It had changed, but it was still there. And always would be. Would Jonas ever be able to understand that? Alanna wondered bleakly. "I do love you, Mitch," she said now, afraid that Jonas might not approve, but feeling that the words had to be said.

"And I love you." He gathered her to him and held her tight, knowing that this would be the last time he'd ever have his arms around her. "But sometimes, Allie, my sweet, love just isn't enough," he added, unwittingly echoing Jonas's words of last night.

They remained that way for a long time, drawing comfort from one another. Finally Alanna tilted back her head. "You never told me where your new assignment is."

"Would it have mattered?" he asked gently.

"No," she admitted. She'd given it a great deal of thought and knew that even if he'd accepted the safety of an anchor job in New York, her life—her future—belonged here with Jonas.

"That's what I thought." He paused, preparing for the explosion. "You're now looking at the network's chief foreign correspondent for Central America."

The explosion came instantaneously. "What?" Alanna was on her feet, staring down at him. "You have to be kidding!"

"Of course I'm not. There's nothing funny about Central America, Allie."

"All the more reason why you have no business going there!" she insisted hotly.

It was almost like old times. They'd been through this before, Mitch recalled. More times than he'd cared to count. Every time he'd decided to go off into forbidden territories, searching out a big story, a scoop, Allie had behaved as if he were hell-bent on committing suicide or something. Back in those days, such disagreements had often escalated into full-blown domestic battles. Now he merely smiled and stood up.

"On the contrary, Allie, my sweet," he argued easily. "I'm a newsman. My business is wherever the news is happening. And right now, a lot of it is happening in Central America."

She stared at him in frustration, knowing all too well the impossibility of changing his mind. "You're going to get yourself killed."

"Never happen." She saw the smile fade from his eyes as he took both her hands into his and looked down at her. "You know, I think I knew from the beginning that you and I weren't going to work out," he admitted. "But I loved you and wanted you so damn badly, I simply ignored all the differences between us."

"I was the same way," Alanna said softly.

"You know what saddens me most about all this?"

Her eyes filled abruptly. "What?" The tears she'd managed to hold off began to stream down her cheeks like a trail of glistening diamonds.

As Mitch tenderly brushed her tears away with his thumbs, he felt his own eyes grow suspiciously moist. "We're not going to get the chance to grow old together."

Alanna almost smiled at that. "You're never going to grow old," she insisted shakily, knowing exactly how Wendy must have felt when she finally had to send Peter

Pan back to Never-Never Land without her. "Because you refuse to grow up."

Mitch wasn't about to deny something he'd thought too many times himself. "I think you may be right." Because he wanted to kiss her, to pull her into his arms and never let go, he backed away. "Since I'm leaving tomorrow, I think it would be better if I spend the night at Mom's."

Alanna nodded. "I packed your things."

So they'd both known. Mitch wasn't surprised. The only surprise was that they'd both waited three long and painful weeks to admit what had been obvious all along. "Thanks. I'll go up and get them."

Upstairs, Mitch looked around the cheery room, knowing that he was seeing it for the last time. If things had been different, if he were a different man, he'd give Jonas Harte a run for his money. But he'd been a newsman long enough to know that facts were facts. And it was high time he faced a few of his own. Sighing, he picked up the suitcase she'd left at the end of the bed.

Alanna was waiting for him at the front door. Just as she had thought of packing his bag ahead of time, she had not been terribly surprised to see that Mitch had kept the limo waiting.

"Take care," she said, swallowing yet another flood of tears as she prepared to watch Mitch walk out of her life.

He grinned, although he felt as though his heart was breaking. "Don't worry. I'm invincible."

The funny thing, Alanna reflected, was that he actually believed it.

"Have a good life, Allie."

"You, too," she whispered. "I'll watch you on the news."

"I'd like that. Knowing that you were watching."

He lowered his head and brushed his lips against her forehead. Then he was gone.

IT WAS DUSK. The sun was setting, streaming ribbons of gold into the dark waters of San Francisco Bay. Gulls dipped and floated over cliff and water; boats rocked gently at their moorings.

Alanna was relieved to find Jonas's boat in its slip. Fortunately, he'd either changed his mind about leaving or had known that she'd be showing up here this evening.

Jonas was sitting out on the deck, waiting for her. He'd seen her park at the end of the pier and take her suitcase out of the car. He'd watched as she made her way toward the boat. Now, as she approached, he wanted to leap out of his deck chair, grab her quickly and pull her into the cabin before she changed her mind. But he remained where he was, allowing her to make the first move.

"Permission to come aboard, Captain?" Although her greeting was bright, he could hear the nervousness.

"Permission granted." He stood up and reached out his hand, helping her onto the boat. The moment her feet touched the deck, Alanna felt as if she was home.

If only she knew what to say. Correction, she knew *what* to say. She didn't know how to say it. All the clever, passionate speeches she'd thought up while driving to Sausalito had fled her mind at the first sight of him. All she could say was what was in her heart.

"Mitch came back today. With the news of a new assignment. In fact, he's leaving for Central America tomorrow."

Brows drawn together, Jonas watched her carefully. "How do you feel about that?"

His calm tone did nothing to soothe her jumpy nerves. Alanna dragged her hand through her hair. "I think it's stupid and foolhardy and irresponsible. I also think that since it's what he wants to do—has to do—then he should do it."

"Alone."

"Yes." That said, she took a deep breath before plunging into more dangerous waters. "Do you still want to marry me, Jonas? Or have I ruined everything?"

He came to her, looking deep into her eyes, seeing how wide and vulnerable they were. Her scent momentarily distracted him, but then he remembered what it was he'd wanted to say. "There's something I should have said when all this first started."

"What?"

"I know you loved Mitch. And I accept that. Because all your feelings for him, your youthful crush, your marriage, the way you fought for his release, then, when it looked like you'd failed, the way you insisted on keeping his memory alive, all those things have made you who you are." He put his hands upon her shoulders. "The woman I love. And I wouldn't want you any other way."

Release bubbled up, cool and sparkling. Alanna fell into his arms. "And I love you."

Jonas pulled her closer. "Tell me again."

"I love you." Alanna laughed as she took his face into her hands. "I love you." She lifted her mouth to his. "Love you," she repeated breathlessly. "And I want to spend the rest of my life making love with you and having your children, and—"

"Hey, wait just a minute," Jonas said, putting her a little away from him. "You can accuse me of being old-fashioned, if you like, but if we're going to have children, shouldn't we manage to fit a wedding in there somewhere?"

"As soon as possible," Alanna agreed. "But for now..." Her mouth found his.

With a groan that was part pleasure, part relief, Jonas scooped her up and carried her into the cabin where they undressed each other with hands that only trembled slightly. And then there was nothing but the pleasure, the joyful, dazzling pleasure of being together again.

It was dark. They lay together in a tangle of arms and legs, finally satiated, finally at peace. Breathing a sigh, Alanna snuggled against Jonas and felt an immense sense of rightness.

"You're awfully quiet," Jonas murmured.

"Mmm."

"What are you thinking about?"

"Oh, this and that." When her gaze shifted to her wedding dress, hanging by the door, waiting to be claimed, Alanna was both excited and calm at the same time. Even more importantly, she felt immensely fulfilled by the path she'd chosen.

"Good thoughts, I hope," Jonas said, nuzzling her neck.

They'd made it. She'd said her farewells, and now it was time for a new beginning. With Jonas. Alanna could hardly wait.

She smiled and lifted her face for his kiss. "The best."

HARLEQUIN Temptation

Lovers Apart

FOUR CONTROVERSIAL STORIES! FOUR DYNAMITE AUTHORS!

Don't miss the LOVERS APART miniseries—four special Temptation books. Look for the third book and the subsequent titles listed below:

March: **Title #340**
MAKING IT by Elise Title

Hannah and Marc . . . Can a newlywed yuppie couple—both partners having demanding careers—find ''time'' for love?

April: **Title #344**
YOUR PLACE OR MINE by Vicki Lewis Thompson

Lila and Bill . . . A divorcée and a widower share a shipboard romance but they're too set in their ways to survive on land!

If you missed January title #332—DIFFERENT WORLDS by Elaine K. Stirling and February title #336—DÉTENTE by Emma Jane Spenser and would like to order them, send your name, address, and zip or postal code, along with a check or money order for $2.65 plus 75¢ postage and handling ($1.00 in Canada) for each book ordered, payable to Harlequin Reader Service, to:

In the U.S.
3010 Walden Ave.
Box 1325
Buffalo, NY 14269-1325

In Canada
P.O. Box 609
Fort Erie, Ontario
L2A 5X3

Please specify book title(s) with your order.
Canadian residents please add applicable federal and provincial taxes.

LAP-3

HARLEQUIN
Romance

This March, travel to Australia with Harlequin Romance's FIRST CLASS title #3110 FAIR TRIAL by Elizabeth Duke.

They came from two different worlds.

Although she'd grown up with a privileged background, Australian lawyer Tanya Barrington had worked hard to gain her qualifications and establish a successful career.

It was unfortunate that she and arrogant barrister Simon Devlin had to work together on a case. He had no time for wealthy socialites, he quickly informed her. Or for women who didn't feel at home in the bush where he lived at every available opportunity. And where he had Tanya meet him to discuss the case.

Their clashes were inevitable—but their attractions to each other was certainly undeniable. . . .

Take 4 bestselling love stories FREE

Plus get a FREE surprise gift!